# NETTLE

# BEX HOGAN

# NETTLE

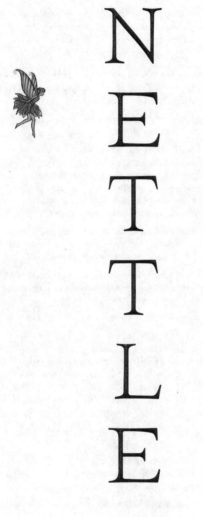

tundra

Originally published in the UK by Zephyr, an imprint of Head of Zeus,
part of Bloomsbury Publishing Plc, 2024

Published in hardcover by Tundra Books, 2025

Text copyright © 2024 by Bex Hogan
Cover art copyright © 2024 by Laura El

Tundra Books, an imprint of Tundra Book Group, a division of
Penguin Random House Canada Ltd., 320 Front Street West,
Suite 1400, Toronto, Ontario, M5V 3B6, Canada

penguinrandomhouse.ca

Published simultaneously in the United States of America by Tundra Books of
Northern New York, an imprint of Tundra Book Group, a division of Penguin
Random House Canada Ltd., P.O. Box 2040, Plattsburgh, NY 12901, USA

Tundra with colophon is a registered trademark of
Penguin Random House Canada Ltd.

All rights reserved. No part of this book may be reproduced, scanned, transmitted,
or distributed in any form or by any electronic or mechanical means, including
information storage and retrieval systems, without permission in writing from the
publisher, except by a reviewer, who may quote brief passages in a review. No part
of this book may be used or reproduced in any manner for the purpose of training
artificial intelligence technologies or systems.

The authorized representative in the EU for product safety and compliance is
Penguin Random House Ireland, Morrison Chambers, 32 Nassau Street,
Dublin D02 YH68, Ireland, https://eu-contact.penguin.ie

*Publisher's note: This book is a work of fiction. Names, characters, places and incidents either
are the product of the author's imagination or are used fictitiously, and any resemblance to
actual persons living or dead, events, or locales is entirely coincidental.*

Library and Archives Canada Cataloguing in Publication

Title: Nettle / Bex Hogan.
Names: Hogan, Bex, author.
Description: Previously published: London: Zephyr, 2024.
Identifiers: Canadiana (print) 20250155109 | Canadiana (ebook) 20250155117 |
ISBN 9781774888759 (hardcover) | ISBN 9781774888766 (EPUB)
Subjects: LCGFT: Fantasy fiction. | LCGFT: Novels.
Classification: LCC PZ7.1.H64 Net 2025 | DDC j823/.92—dc23

Library of Congress Control Number: 2025932860

Cover design by Jessie Price / Head of Zeus
Typeset by Ed Pickford
The text was set in Agmena Pro Book
Interior illustrations by Jessie Price

Printed in Canada

1 2 3 4 5      29 28 27 26 25

For Fiona.
So you can escape to Faery
whenever you wish.

# ONE

 nce there was a girl called Nettle. She was all things wild, with a sting to boot. At night she dreamed of silver bells singing her name.

Once there was a girl called Nettle. She was all things prickly and untamed. Voices whispered to her from the darkness.

Once there was a girl called Nettle. She was all things dangerous and laced with magic. The faeries stole her away to their world.

Once there was a girl called Nettle. And that girl was me.

It wasn't always my name, I used to have another. But it didn't belong to me.

The first time my grandma found me lying in a patch of nettles, she dragged me out by my hair, tangled like a thorny thicket even then, and frantically checked my bare arms and legs for any sign of a rash. When she found none, she'd looked at me, bewildered.

"They didn't hurt you?" In her surprise, her words almost sounded like an accusation. I'd shaken my head and we'd gone inside for lemonade.

The second time, she'd been calmer, yet I saw panic in her eyes.

The third time she asked me why I kept doing it, why I kept lying among the green leaves. I remember my answer so clearly.

*Because I feel safe there.*

And from that day forward, no one ever called me anything else. Nettle was my name and my nature.

"You know why they grow?" Grandma would ask when I played among the coarse stalks. "Because the faeries are near. The threshold between our two worlds, that thin veil that keeps us separated, is marked by nettles. They warn us and protect us."

I think she thought the name would protect me too.

Or perhaps she simply hoped.

Our little cottage was as crooked as they came. Perched on a hill that had open moorland in one direction and dense forest in the other, it gave us everything we needed. Enough land to grow food, to graze animals. A world that was entirely ours, created by my grandma to make me happy.

It had always been just the two of us, living in nature's embrace. When I was younger, I'd once asked about my parents, more out of curiosity than anything else, but the blood had drained from Grandma's face and concern had clouded her eyes. Then she had swept me into her arms and joked that only the faeries could have left such a child behind. I had beamed and tucked the thought away, letting it rise whenever I sought comfort for being different from the children in the village.

Grandma was my tutor as well as my guardian. "Schools don't teach you what really matters," she would say, but we both knew that wasn't why she kept me home. The village whispers were far from quiet. We heard them well enough. I didn't care though, it simply meant I never had to leave her, and between letters and numbers, Grandma taught me to understand the trees, the flowers, the weeds. She showed me how to weave baskets from willow, to turn sloes to wine, to use heather as a natural dye. I would roam the moors and collect sheep's fleece from the barbed wire fencing, watching as she washed, then carded my finds, before sitting, mesmerized, at her feet as she fed it into her spinning wheel, transforming it to yarn. She raised me on a diet of botany, crafts, and most importantly, myth.

To her, faery lore was as real as history and oh, how I adored listening to her stories of rival courts, gowns spun from shadow, endless dancing beneath scarlet stars. A place of danger and deception but more beauty than I could dare imagine. Yet for all the reverence with which she spoke about the fae and their world, her warnings were not to be ignored. *Do not venture into the forest. Ignore the voices on the wind. Stay on the moorland paths and stray for nothing.*

The fierce blaze in her eyes when she'd held me by my shoulders and issued these rules had burned through me and I'd heeded them as if they were the laws of nature itself.

How I wished her eyes would glow like that now. She hadn't opened them since yesterday, her breath rattling in her chest. I held her hand tightly in my own.

"Please, Grandma," I said. "Let me call the doctor again."

She shook her head, barely a fraction. No more doctors. We'd already had this conversation before she'd deteriorated.

*There's nothing more they can do. That anyone can do.*

There was something I could do though, something to offer her a morsel of comfort. I lifted her hand and pressed it to my cheek.

"Once many long moons ago and beneath a starry sky, the king and queen of the faery realms pledged their love to one another and united their two kingdoms.

Such a joyous union demanded the most lavish of feasts, and all the fae-folk joined the celebration, delighting in the endless dishes of sugared fruits and pastries so light they practically floated into hungry mouths. Goblets overflowed with the sweetest wines and all the world was merriment.

"When they'd had their fill at the banquet table, the king and queen declared there should be music. And so there was, the most mellifluous music ever heard, and the revelers watched in wonder as the bride and groom spun in each other's arms. The pair vowed fidelity and trust, and above all pledged to forever keep peace in their lands."

I paused. This was my grandma's favorite of all her many faery stories, one filled with love and joy, but tonight it seemed to be causing her more distress than solace.

"What is it?" I asked softly. "Do you want me to tell you a different one?"

A tear trailed over her cheek toward her ear. "I'm sorry," she said, a sob that I scarcely caught.

"You have nothing to be sorry for," I said, kissing the papery skin of her hand. "Nothing at all."

"Because of me, you never danced beneath the stars."

"Then you've not been paying attention," I said with a smile. "Because I dance out there most nights."

"Alone." Another tear slid from her eye. "And when I'm gone, you'll have no one."

"You're still here," I reminded her. "You don't have to worry about me."

I stayed with her until she fell into a fretful sleep and then made my way through the quiet house, down the narrow stairs. There were chores for me to do before going to bed and I set about them in an attempt to suppress the growing dread that swelled in my chest.

I didn't want to think about what my grandma had said, didn't want to imagine my life without her in it. And yet it was becoming harder to ignore.

She was right. I would be alone.

There were no friends to lean on. When I was younger, I had briefly been befriended by some of the village girls, who fell in love with our world on the hill. They adored riding my pony, feeding the ducks, plucking ripe raspberries from the canes. Their parents approved of them playing outside, even if they raised an eyebrow because I was filthy compared to their daughters. They would never have been permitted to roam the moors alone in the moonlight or bring abandoned fox cubs home to raise. For a time, all was well. Until I started to tell them about the faeries.

They hadn't heard any of Grandma's stories before, so I shared my favorites. I explained how they should leave gifts for the faeries, to show respect. The creamy top of the milk and bread dipped in honey, placed on the doorstep on a frosty morning. A drizzle of wine poured across the ground. A pebble decorated with a colorful pattern.

When they all wanted a token to offer the faeries, I made up tiny bundles for them to take home, twigs, dried flowers, and rodent bones tied with a pretty hair ribbon. I was so proud of those little gifts, imagining how happy the faeries would be to receive them.

The parents, however, did not share my excitement—apparently, bones weren't appropriate for children. After that the girls stopped coming to play, and when I ventured to the village in search of company, the friends who had once danced with me turned away.

They laughed as I wandered barefoot along the pavement, recoiled when a spider crawled from my hair and scuttled down my arm so I could rehome it in a hedgerow. They shouted names at me as I bowed in reverence to the trees I passed. To begin with their taunts hurt and so I cheered myself up by playing tricks on them. I left baskets of toffee apples on their doorsteps—only beneath the caramel was raw onion. Then doughnuts—filled with mayonnaise instead of custard. One girl had chickens in her back garden, and so I slipped in early before the morning sun and switched half the fresh eggs for smooth brown rocks.

Soon I had fully established a reputation for being a troublemaker, but I realized I didn't care what any of those people thought of me. I had Grandma. I didn't need anyone else.

"And I have you," I said to my chickens as I ushered them back to the safety of their coop for the night. The door of their henhouse was loose, so I took my penknife from my pocket, using it as a makeshift screwdriver to fix the hinge.

Once they were secure, I rounded up the runner ducks, before heading to the orchard to catch Bracken and Moss. The days of chasing them round the field were long gone, both my pony and his donkey companion far too old to do much more than plod. The lure of the warm stables was irresistible to them.

As I walked through the chill of the evening air, a breeze whipped up, carrying a whisper to me.

*Nettle.*

The voice was not unfamiliar. I'd heard it calling my name for as long as I could remember, a twilight lament heralding the coming darkness. I'd never told Grandma, not after the way she'd reacted when I'd mentioned I dreamed of bells, their eerie melody seeming to ring my name. She rarely raised her voice, but her frightened rebuke then had stung as though she'd struck me.

The hairs on the back of my neck rose as the breeze intensified, before dying away. I stood for a moment, almost dizzy with disquiet, before I gathered myself and carried on to the orchard, where Bracken and Moss waited patiently for me at the gate.

"You're a disgrace to your ancestors," I told Bracken as I bolted the stable door shut. "Honestly, you wouldn't last five minutes on the moor."

Grandma had bought him for me at the market when I was little. He was getting on a bit even then, but I'd spent more hours of my childhood with him than anyone else. Galloping across the moorland on a native pony was magical.

He nuzzled my arm, expectantly. "You're spoiled, do you know that?" I asked, taking an apple from my pocket and slicing it in half. As he took the fruit, I stroked his nose affectionately and tried not to let my mind wander toward morbid thoughts. Like Grandma, Bracken wouldn't be with me forever.

With a last check that he had all he needed, I gave Moss the other half of the apple, and satisfied he was comfortable too, went to fill the watering cans outside.

As I was leaving the barn, the pile of old horseshoes caught my eye. Grandma was as superstitious as she was devout to the old ways. Hawthorn was forbidden in the house, white heather and bluebells must never be picked, and on Midsummer's Eve all the mirrors were covered for fear a glimpse at our reflection on such a night would allow the faeries to steal us away. She needn't have bothered, I rarely paused to study myself in a looking glass. I knew what I would see: a permanently pale complexion, no matter how many hours spent in the sun; sharp features that falsely suggested a talent for cunning; hazel eyes, each with a circle of green flecks like a spring wreath; wild not-quite-black, not-quite-brown hair.

We kept the horseshoes both for good luck and to guard the house and stables from roaming evil—they hung over every external doorway. It occurred to me as I stared at them that there could be no harm in putting another above my grandma's bed. She needed all the help she could get, so I picked the nicest-looking and slipped it into one of my pockets. While I liked to imagine myself in elaborate faery gowns of silk that dazzled like stardust, I opted for loose, practical dresses instead. I sewed my own from linen and ensured they had deep pockets for occasions such as this.

As I rounded the shed, my dress caught on a nail and ripped.

I cursed. This was my newest one, but I guessed having to repair it was some sort of clothing rite-of-passage. Heaven forbid I own something not torn and endlessly mended.

Once the garden was watered, both flower and vegetable patches, I headed to my favorite place: the unkempt border of our land at the bottom of the hill, which marked the place where the wilderness ended and our haven began. It was here the nettles grew, in dense clumps. I waded through them and settled myself among the green leaves, their hairs tickling me harmlessly. The purpose of having such roomy pockets in my dress was so that I could carry necessities with me at all times, saving me from traipsing in and out of the house. A small sewing kit absolutely fell under that category and I pulled it out, swiftly setting about the repair.

The light was fading fast, and I knew what Grandma would say if she saw me.

*You'll ruin your eyes doing that in such poor light.*

It never bothered me. Working by the sun or moon was all the same, my keen eyes adjusting well to the shift. And honestly? I enjoyed basking in the moon's caress, pretending it was silvery starlight I stitched through my material rather than common thread.

When my dress was fixed, I lay flat to gaze at the night sky. I should go back to the house, check Grandma didn't need anything, get some sleep before another day began. But I'd made a mistake. I'd stopped. Keeping going was the only thing that had prevented the shadows from invading my mind.

The truth could no longer be ignored. Grandma was going to die. I would have no one. Much as I enjoyed my own company, craved independence, and cherished the land we lived on, the prospect of losing her left an aching hollow in my chest.

"Please," I begged the gathering darkness. "Please don't let her die."

My fingers trailed across the nettles before clenching them in my fists, sorrow and rage entwined.

"Please." My plea came from the deepest part of me.

The faint ringing of bells carried through the dusk. The same sound I heard in my dreams. *The call of the faeries*, my grandma had said. *Don't listen to it*, she'd warned. *Turn away from the sound.*

She feared them, but I feared losing her more.

Clutching the nettles more tightly, I closed my eyes. "If you can save her, I'll do anything."

The bells rang louder, the wind whipped wildly, my untamed locks dancing to its tune. And my whole world fell away.

# TWO

Falling. Flying. Fast and fleeting. A directionless movement that made my head spin.

When at last it stopped, I opened my eyes.

I no longer recognized the sky above me. It was violet, a fitting backdrop for the two vast moons, one crimson, the other silver, that held court over the myriad scarlet stars.

Blinking did nothing to disperse the scene. Wherever I was, it wasn't my garden.

Scrambling to my feet, I realized the only thing that was the same was the nettle patch that surrounded me. The hill and my home were gone, and though a forest loomed beside me, and open moorland stretched the other way, there was scant resemblance to the landscape I'd grown up in. Panic burned like bile in my throat.

"Grandma?" I called, though it was hopeless. "Grandma!" Silence was my only reply. Wherever I was, she was far from my reach. I had to get back to her. She was too ill to be left alone, what would happen when she woke and I wasn't there? What if she died without me by her side to breathe well wishes for her onward journey? What if I never saw her again?

Such thoughts nearly paralyzed me. If I was to find my way home though, I needed to push them somewhere deep inside where they couldn't hinder me. And I *had* to find my way home.

The obvious thing to do was to reverse what had been done. I lay back in the nettles and closed my eyes.

"Please." I fought to keep my voice steady. "Let me go home." I grasped the nettles, trying to replicate what I'd done before. But there were no bells. No whispers. The ground did not move and I remained where I was.

Was it possible? Could I have been heard by the fae folk? Had I really fallen into another world?

"You fool," I muttered. Had I not had enough warnings? What was I thinking calling to the fae?

*Nettle.*

The voice drifted softly from the forest. The same one I'd heard not that long ago at home. Here it had a very different effect, swirling around me, settling possessively onto my skin. It acted like a siren's call, drawing me toward the treeline. I stumbled forwards, desperate to hear it again.

The sound of thundering hooves broke the strange enchantment, bringing me to my senses. Galloping fast toward me were half a dozen horses with eyes like blood diamonds, their flowing manes reaching almost to their knees, so that their riders had knotted stirrups into the hair. They had no tack, the warriors riding bareback holding weapons rather than reins. But it was their bared teeth, filed to lethal points that made me run. The forest might have the whispering voice, but I would take that over the terrifying horses and hollering riders pounding my way.

It was futile, of course. I could not possibly outrun such creatures, and they soon overtook me, rearing to a halt and blocking my path to the relative sanctuary of the forest. The riders were even more fearsome up close, the eerie red light bouncing off their hairless heads and illuminating their ears, which were as pointed as their teeth.

"Stop, spy," they growled, aiming spears made of carved bone at my face.

I raised my hands in self-defense or surrender. I didn't know which. "I'm no spy," I gasped, fighting to keep my voice steady. "I'm just lost."

The strange sound they made might have been laughter; it was impossible to tell. "Save your lies for the king," their leader said.

"I'm not lying, all I want is to go home," I promised.

The riders hissed in anger.

"To report back to the queen? Never!" Another of the warriors closed in on me, his eyes flashing with fury. "You're coming with us."

I had no choice, that much was obvious, but it didn't stop me kicking and screaming as the rider grabbed my arm in his clawlike fingers and hauled me up onto the horse in front of him, so that I lay on my stomach as we set off at a pace faster than anything Bracken had ever managed.

Frantically, I tried to snatch at air, but it was hard to fill my lungs in such a position, the ground flying past so swiftly I had to close my eyes to ease the sickness. *Think*, I urged myself. Whoever these riders were, it sounded like they were taking me to see their king. Perhaps he would be able to help me — once I had convinced him I wasn't a spy, or whatever else they thought I was. If I wasn't dreaming, if I really *had* fallen into another realm, then I had to remember everything Grandma had ever told me — and hope her stories were right. Only hours ago, I'd told her the tale of the faery king and queen's wedding — was it possible I was on my way to their court now?

Twisting my head, I tried to see where we were going . . . but there was nothing beyond open moorland. My heart sank. I didn't think I could bear to go much further like this. Then I caught a glimpse of something ahead and shifted my weight to get a better look. Tiny buds formed on the horizon, growing into mounds as we approached at impossible speed, until rolling hillsides loomed before us. Glittering rivers cascaded down some, ancient forests sprawled across others, but they couldn't draw my gaze away from the palace perched on the highest hill. It was a black silhouette against the violet night sky, all thin towers and pointed turrets, but it bewitched me nevertheless. Clusters of scarlet stars burst above it like fireworks released to celebrate our arrival. Beneath it, a town spread like rambling roots seeking to anchor the palace in place.

That was where we were going. My fingers wound instinctively in the horse's mane, clinging on as it covered the ground faster than should have been possible.

Soon we were ascending the hills, weaving along an invisible path toward the outskirts of the town. Then we flew past stone walls, a blur of huts and buildings, and all the while the distant clamor grew louder, until it drowned the thunder of the horses' hooves.

"The Night Riders are here!"

The shout rose over the noise, and I tried to look about as the horses slowed to a brisk trot.

We had reached the heart of the bustling town, the crowd parting for the horses as we rode along cobbled streets, illuminated by many lanterns. The smells were intoxicating, floral perfumes and spices blended with earthiness and wood. The smoky scent of roasting chestnuts mingled with the coppery tang of sizzling meat. Behind the throng of voices, music was playing, so giddy and infectious that even in my precarious situation, my feet began to move in time to the rhythm.

It was as busy as if it was daytime, but we weren't here to purchase food or wares. The horses continued to climb toward the stone walls beyond the market, and as the incline leveled, we reached a grand gateway that looked at first to be made of pale wrought iron, but then I realized it was antlers twisted and bound by creeping ivy.

The gates opened to permit us entrance and, to my great relief, the horses came to a halt. I was pulled from my uncomfortable position and faltered as my feet touched the ground, only staying upright because the rider who'd captured me gripped my arms so tightly.

"This way," he said, pushing me forwards, as I took in the sight before me.

The palace.

Up close, it was even more magical, and my breath caught in my throat. It was an impossible structure, formed of trees and roots, boughs and branches, moss and lichen, stone and bone, leaves and berries. It looked as alive as any creature, but strong and ancient. Above the entrance, sinister faces of gnarled wood watched our approach. It was simultaneously threatening and ethereal, and left me in no doubt.

I truly was in the land of the faeries.

The Night Riders escorted me through a gorse archway and into a corridor carpeted with spongy heather, which led to the throne room. Skeletal trees stripped of bark shaped the room, towering to offer support to a canopy of hanging wild clematis. Roots erupted from the ground to provide an entwined base for the vast granite throne, and my eyes slowly rose to take in the exquisite man sitting upon it.

His pants were made of leather and stitched with silver leaves, his arms covered by tendrils of ivy that seemed to grow from his skin. His chest was bare, as smooth as polished marble yet glittering like starlight. Pointed ears poked through the long black hair that hung past his shoulders, framing his perfect features. Strong jaw, high cheekbones, piercing eyes. Upon his head sat a crown of hawthorn twigs, shaped to give the appearance of many antlers, reminiscent of the gateway, and decorated with moss and lichen, sparkling with dewdrops.

He sniffed the air and his expression turned to one of disgust.

"You dare bring a human into my presence?" Even outraged, his voice was alluring, deep, and melodic. "I will not look on her."

I waited for the Night Riders to respond, but nothing happened. Then I realized the king hadn't been addressing them, but countless spiders, which were now descending from the branches framing the ceiling. They were the size of thimbles, silver-white and ghostlike and, as they dropped, a skein of finest web fell upon my head covering my face. To my surprise, I could see clearly through the silky gauze as the Night Riders shoved me closer to the throne. The veil obviously served some purpose, because the king deigned to look at me directly.

"What possible reason could you have for bringing *this* before me?" he asked the Night Riders. Disdain dripped from his voice.

"Found her near the border, Your Majesty," the Night Rider leader replied. "She was running back toward the forest."

"A spy," the king said, an edge to his voice. "What shall we do with her?"

Murmurs echoed off the walls of the hall as if it was filled with people.

"Burn her!"

"Torture her!"

"Sacrifice!"

The words were brimming with gleeful venom, each a tiny prick to my skin, and I knew if I didn't say something quickly, I was going to be punished as some kind of traitor.

"I'm not a spy!" I shouted, silencing the cruel chorus.

The king tilted his head, catlike, eyes burning with incredulity.

"You dare speak without my permission?"

"I'm sorry," I said. "It's just it sounded like you were going to kill me and I'd really rather not die, especially for something I haven't done."

There was a collective holding of breath as the Night Riders waited to see what response my outburst would receive. Had I sealed my fate rather than saving myself?

The king rose to his feet and came down from his throne, his presence more intimidating with every step. When he was an arm's length away, he stopped, as if not wanting to be any closer to me. "Do you know how fortunate you are still to draw breath, mortal? I despise your kind, and though the spiders' work protects me from having to look upon you, it will not protect you. So answer me once and for all, what are you?"

"I'm no one. I was in my garden, lying in a bed of nettles, pleading to anyone who would listen to save my grandmother and then I fell and found myself here. This is all a terrible mistake and I want to go home." The words spilled out, catching in my throat as fear and exhaustion threatened to overwhelm me.

His dark eyes shone with unexpected emotion. "Keita," he breathed, his voice tinged with sadness. When he spoke again, any trace of sorrow was gone. "She must have heard your cry and summoned you. She always did have an inexplicable fondness for your kind. Tell me, what did my queen say?"

It was hard to pay attention to his words, the timbre of his voice so beguiling.

"I heard only bells."

His eyes narrowed. "Bells?" With a discerning gaze, he walked slowly around me. "You are hiding something. Tell me."

"I'm not," I insisted. "Truly."

My answer disappointed him. "Take her away."

"No!"

The Night Riders grabbed my arms and started to pull me away. My heart pounded in my chest, I had to do something. "Wait, please! I have to go home, I'll do anything."

The second time tonight I'd offered such a ridiculous promise. It hadn't worked out well before.

The king raised his hand and the Night Riders released me. He beckoned me to approach, signaling when I was close enough. His expression had changed, every feature calculating, and I imagined this was how my chickens felt in the face of a cunning fox about to steal into their coop.

"Anything?" he asked.

What choice did I have? I had nowhere to run. "All I want is to save my grandma and go home to her. So yes, I will do anything for that to happen."

The light that burned in his eyes betrayed any attempt at casual indifference. He was a hunter who had perfectly cornered his prey.

"What you ask is simple enough," he said. "With a mere click of my fingers I can grant what you desire. But not for nothing." His eyes flickered to mine, and although I knew he could not see them, I felt their intense scrutiny nonetheless. "Complete three tasks for me and I shall give you what you ask."

So many stories Grandma had told me involved faeries making deals with humans, which were never wise and always dangerous. But hope rose within me at his words.

"You really can heal her? And I can return to her?"

The king nodded. "If you complete my three tasks. You need only give your word for the contract to be binding, so tell me, human, do we have a deal?"

My instincts screamed at me not to be enticed by such temptation, but . . . Grandma. I would do anything for her.

"We have a deal."

"Well then," he said, "welcome to my court. I am Locryn, King of the Moorland, and you are now in my service."

# THREE

His words settled on me like the first winter frost and I shivered. What had I done? A deal with a faery? Was I determined to disregard all the advice my grandma had ever given me? And yet, I was doing this for her. It would be fine, I convinced myself. I would do as he asked and everything would go back to normal.

Locryn dismissed the Night Riders with a flick of his wrist, before returning to his throne, throwing his legs to hang over the side. "Ellion," he said, and at his summons a man in a long robe emerged from the shadows. Had he always been there, or had he just appeared? "Put her somewhere I shan't be troubled by her presence."

"Of course, Your Majesty," Ellion said, bowing.

"Wait," I said, sensing I was about to be dismissed. "What about my tasks?"

Locryn waved his hand again. "All in good time."

"My grandma doesn't have time on her side. And . . ." A horrible thought occurred to me. "My animals have no one to look after them."

"Enough." The word was a clear warning. "I am time's master. Should I give the word, time can stand still between our worlds. It can also be made to move faster or allowed to trickle at the same speed. You had better hope I am not provoked to act against your interests."

Ellion took me by the elbow and this time I didn't resist as he escorted me from the throne room. When we neared the doorway, I stole a glance back toward Locryn and was unnerved to see him staring at me intently. His expression was more malicious than benign, and I looked away.

Once I was beyond the king's sight, my veil disintegrated. Ellion, who held my arm lightly but firmly, said nothing, but I took the opportunity to look at him more closely. Though not quite as beautiful as his king, he was undoubtedly handsome, as if his face too had been sculpted to perfection. His brown skin was flawless, his features refined. His black hair wasn't as long as Locryn's, though it fell to his shoulders and was flecked with silver, like scattered stardust. How old was he? I was terrible at judging people's ages but I was certain that although he looked a similar age to me, he was much, much older.

"My name is Ellion," he said, perhaps aware of my gaze. "And you are?"

A memory tugged inside me that to tell a faery your name would give them power over you. I could hardly ignore him, so I offered a half-truth. "Felicity," I said, giving the name my grandma had once called me long ago.

Ellion regarded me and frowned. "No," he said after a beat. "That's not your name."

I met his gaze, intending to be defiant, but instead I stared at the faint silver rings in his otherwise dark brown eyes. They reminded me of my own flecked irises, and that hint of familiarity weakened my defenses. "I'm Nettle."

He nodded, hearing the truth in my reply. "Welcome to the court," he said, his voice lacking the required warmth for such a greeting. "While you are a guest here at the king's pleasure, should you need anything you are to call me. I am a shadow faery, so as long as there are shadows cast close by, I will hear you."

"Okay," I said, but noted his obvious displeasure at having to be at my service. I wouldn't be bothering him unless absolutely necessary.

I was soon distracted by the change in my surroundings. Ellion led me into another hallway, this time made of granite, ivy creeping through the cracks. Arched windows were positioned too high for me to see through, and the candles of countless candelabras dripped wax, which melted into the air before hitting the stone floor.

At the far end of the long corridor was a narrow wooden door. It opened at Ellion's approach and he gestured for me to go through. I was outside again, but this time there was no market, no hubbub. Instead, there was the most charming garden I had ever seen, filled with flowers that bloomed in the starlight, fountains that glittered, hedges clipped into whimsical shapes that, from the corner of my eye, seemed to dance and twirl. There was no time to take it all in, as Ellion marched swiftly to a courtyard beyond which something was, at last, familiar. Stables, barns, the sweetly sour scent of manure.

He took me to the far corner of the yard and gestured to a stall.

"You can sleep here," he said. "When the king has need of you, I will return."

I stared at the empty stable, with nothing but a pile of straw heaped at the sides. "What am I supposed to do until then?"

"That is of no interest to me," Ellion replied, before striding across the quiet yard and vanishing into the shadows.

Alone for the first time since I'd arrived in this kingdom, I was hit by a wave of exhaustion. Despite the late hour, I could still hear the faint hum of music and chatter wafting from beyond the palace walls. The market clearly never slept. I, on the other hand, really needed to.

There was no lantern, so I left the stall door open while I shook the straw into a bed I could lie on. Then I pulled the bottom half of the door shut, before settling on my dusty mattress.

*What have you done?* I asked myself as I lay there. Not only did I allow the faeries to steal me away to their land, but I'd made a deal with their king. I had to be smarter than that if I wanted to succeed in my tasks and get home to Grandma. My hands rummaged in my deep pockets and I sighed with relief. Amazingly, nothing had fallen out on my ride here — sewing kit, horseshoe, penknife, string, bandages, and half a bag of lemon sherbets. I took one of the candies and sucked on it, knowing it wouldn't appease my grumbling stomach, but it was better than nothing. Perhaps in the morning Ellion would bring me something to eat. Grandma had told enough tales warning that faery food binds you to their world, never to escape. The king's promise was surely more powerful though. And I would have to eat eventually.

Sleep seemed unlikely in such uncomfortable surroundings, nonetheless I soon found myself drifting off, and the last thing I remembered was the sound of that voice calling me once more.

*Nettle.*

I woke with a start. My hands rested on the straw and everything flooded back to me. It hadn't been a dream then. I was very much still in a stable in the court of the Moorland Faery King.

Someone cleared their throat and I scrambled to sit up.

In the doorway, a young man was silhouetted against the morning light, leaning on a pitchfork.

"You're not a horse," he said.

Hurrying to my feet and brushing the errant stalks of straw from my dress, I shielded my eyes against the sun so I could see him better. Though he looked about my age, he was dressed as if he'd stepped out of a history book. With his filthy, tattered breeches, his once white shirt untucked, and his crop of dark tousled hair, he looked like an eighteenth-century stable boy. But most importantly, he looked distinctly human.

"And you're not a faery."

He didn't look amused. "Good. Now that's settled, can you go somewhere else so I can do my work?"

"I was told I should sleep here," I said in my defense, noting the ghost of an Irish accent in his voice.

"Who told you?" he asked with undisguised irritation.

"I did."

We both jumped as Ellion appeared from the shadowy corner of the stall. The young man dipped his head, respectfully.

"Sorry, I didn't realize," he said to the shadow faery, whose power seemed to fill the small space. "I'll find somewhere else to put Alla."

The stable boy cast me a quick glance, his expression unreadable. He left, and I was alone with Ellion once more.

"The king has decided your first task," he said, without preamble. "Fill this with nettles from the woodland that borders the palace to the west." He handed me a hessian bag along with a knife in a leather sleeve. "They must be cut beneath the two moons. When you have succeeded, bring them to the throne room to present to the king."

A sense of relief rushed through me. That didn't sound too hard, I could do that. "Just this sack?" I asked.

Ellion flashed a wicked grin. "Just that one sack."

"I'll do it tonight," I said, wanting — *needing* — him to know I was serious about this. That I would undertake my work as swiftly as possible.

"We shall see," he said and stepped back to allow the shadows to swallow him.

Frowning, I looked more closely at the items he'd given me. The sack was utterly unremarkable, but the knife was carved from bone, like the spearheads the Night Riders had pointed at me. There were some markings carved into it, but not in any language I recognized. Returning it to its sheath, I slipped the blade into my pocket and folded the sack up in the corner of the stable for later. Assuming faery days were much the same length as human ones, it would be a while until nightfall, so I decided it would be wise to try to find the woodland Ellion had spoken of. That way I wouldn't waste the moonlit hours. I had to get back to Grandma as soon as possible.

The first thing that hit me as I left the stable was the difference in light. This world was washed faintly pink. The violet sky had faded to lilac, the vast sun a warm rose gold. At home, a sky like this at sunrise would herald a shepherd's warning, but here it was entirely a delight.

While the yard had been empty when I'd arrived, now the stables were occupied with the Night Riders' intimidating steeds. At the far end, one of them was tied outside its stall, where the young man who had woken me was busy grooming it.

Anxiety spiked in my chest. I wasn't good at talking to people, it was awkward and uncomfortable and never ended the way I expected. But I was a stranger in a strange land. After a moment's hesitation, I headed toward him.

The horse looked far less intimidating without its rider. Its coat shone in the rosy light, as the young man rubbed it with a wisp of straw. As I approached, I realized the horse's eyes weren't red, but crystal-like, reflecting whatever light they found. Currently they were like two amethysts set in an ebony skull.

"Hi," I said shyly, wondering how best to begin. "Do you need any help?"

He glanced at me. "Only a stable for Alla."

That threw me. Should I leave? "I'm Nettle. Do you have a name?"

"Conor," he replied. "What are you doing here? Morcan didn't mention anything about bringing in another servant."

"Oh, no," I said, wondering who Morcan might be. "I'm new."

"Obviously." His tone was icy.

"No, I mean to this place. I fell through a portal last night and—"

"You're *new*?" he gasped.

I smiled. "That's what I said."

In light of this revelation, his hostility faded.

"I'm sorry," he said. "For the life you've lost."

"That's okay," I said, trying to pretend the lump in my throat wasn't there. "I won't be here long hopefully."

Conor paused what he was doing, glancing sharply at me. His eyes were a startling blue. "What makes you think that?"

He was impossible to read and I had no idea whether I should confide in him. The king hadn't stated our deal was a secret, but what if I wasn't supposed to say anything? I couldn't risk angering Locryn.

"Well, they can't keep us here forever, can they?" I said lightly. "How long has it been for you?"

The haunted look in his eyes silenced me and I ran my hand along the horse's neck, cursing myself for my clumsy attempt to change the conversation.

"Please tell me you didn't do anything stupid," he said.

I refused to meet his searching gaze. "Of course not."

"Really? You haven't done something you'll regret, like make a deal with the king?"

My heart forgot how to beat, but I kept any emotion from my face. "What would be so bad about that?" I asked as nonchalantly as possible.

Conor gave me a knowing look, and I hated how my reddening cheeks betrayed me.

He shrugged. "Nothing," he replied. "I have a deal with him myself."

"You do?" His wry smile caught me off guard.

"Yes. One task is all I have to complete to earn my freedom and return home." He gestured toward two barns at the end of the yard. "I have to move all the straw from that barn, into the other."

"That's it?" I frowned, wondering when he'd made such an easy deal.

"Sounds simple, doesn't it? Except no matter how hard I try, no matter how close I come to succeeding, the first barn always ends up full again. It isn't just a task he gave me—it's an impossible task." Conor watched me across the horse's back and I knew he saw my fear as clearly as I saw his pity. "Don't make the same mistake I did."

I blinked twice, to hold back threatening tears. I couldn't fall apart now. But there was also no point denying the truth.

"I think it's too late for that."

# FOUR

Conor shook his head. "You fool."

I bristled at his insult. "No more than you."

"I'd been here a lot longer than a few hours when I made my deal. I was desperate."

"*I'm* desperate," I shot back. "You don't know anything about me." I was only angry because he was right. I was a fool. "It was a trick," I whispered, thinking of Grandma and how I had failed her entirely.

"They're faeries," Conor said, bitterness coiled around the words. "Of course it was a trick."

"Then that makes the deal worthless? We can renegotiate."

Conor raised an eyebrow. "The deal still holds. Locryn would honor the agreement if we could actually complete our tasks. He's simply rigged the game to ensure that we can't. So I hope you like your stable, because you're going to be there for a very long time."

I wasn't sure what threw me most, the hopelessness of our situation, or Conor's animosity. It shouldn't have been a surprise to me and yet the realization that at home or here, I was apparently fundamentally unlikeable, hurt.

Well, who cared? When had I ever let other people push me from my path? Why should I believe him anyway? For all I knew, he was part of the trickery, to prevent me from completing my tasks. No, I wouldn't give up so easily. If the king wanted a sack full of nettles, he would get a sack full of nettles.

"How do I reach the woodland west of here?" I asked Conor, who seemed taken aback at my out-of-nowhere question. Perhaps he saw the glint in my eyes as I found my resolve, or maybe he was glad of a way to be rid of me, but he gestured to the end of the yard.

"Keep going round to the right, there's an exit out of the palace back into the town. You'll have to take the south road for a while before it forks toward the west wood."

I nodded my thanks and started to walk away.

"Why do you want to know?" he called after me. When I didn't answer, he added, "Are you seriously going to go without any shoes?"

Still ignoring him, I diverted briefly into the stable to retrieve the sack, which I tucked under my arm, before heading on my way. I wasn't entirely sure I could trust his directions, but it was somewhere to start.

The path was overgrown, gorse clawing at my legs as I brushed past. I soon saw the crumbling stone archway in the outer wall. I had to clamber through thick ivy and a tangle of honeysuckle to reach it, my fingers grazing across the rough granite as I slipped free from the palace.

The ground was stony, but I'd spent my whole life walking barefoot so it didn't bother me and I made swift progress toward the town, which was now quiet, a sleepy place bathed in the pinkish light that reminded me of sunrise back home.

Once I reached a proper road, I welcomed the smoothness of the cobbles beneath my feet and took a moment to get my bearings. The road was flanked by the most startling hedgerows, similar to those on my own moorlands, but not bound by the same laws of nature. Hawthorn and blackthorn grew side by side, the red haws unnaturally striking beside the white blackthorn blossom. Wild rose threaded itself among them, covered simultaneously with delicate pink flowers and scarlet hips. And woven throughout was Old Man's Beard, giving the illusion that clouds had floated to earth and been caught in the thicket.

At the foot of the hedgerows were banks of campions, primroses, and bluebells, and carpets of dandelions, some in flower, others turned to seed. I stooped to pick a dandelion clock. Grandma had called them faery clocks when I was little. I'd always made a wish with every puff to set the seeds free. I closed my eyes and blew.

*I wish I was home.*

When I opened my eyes, I was still in the same place. Wishing was as futile here as back in my world.

Though this wasn't the road I'd arrived on with the Night Riders, I was fairly certain that to head back down the hill would lead me to where the market sprawled. So presumably the other direction was south as Conor had advised, and I followed it, hoping I'd soon catch a glimpse of the trees I was seeking.

Silence was my only companion and it was then I became aware of the absence of birdsong. The skies were still, no rustling of wings in the hedgerow. Perhaps there wasn't enough light to wake the birds, or maybe they didn't exist here. Whatever the reason, I missed their presence.

It wasn't long before I reached the brow of the hill and discovered the secrets beyond. The hedgerows gave way to an unexpected row of houses that seemed entirely out of place, woodland towering in the distance.

Relieved to be going the right way, I continued along the street, entranced by the buildings. Each was freestanding and crooked. They were tall and thin, as if someone had come along and stretched them one by one, but what was most captivating was the way they were covered from top to bottom in flowers. Some were buried under rambling roses, with perfect blooms in every shade imaginable. Others were adorned by clematis, with flowers as big as dinner plates, or trailing honeysuckle, wisteria, and jasmine. The scent was intoxicating. It took me back to heady summer days drinking in the garden's luxurious perfume, and something inside me eased at the memory. Urgency gave way to serenity. There was far too much beauty here to suspect any danger, and I was possessed by the urge to linger a while.

I wandered toward the nearest house bejeweled with roses the color of twilight, wanting to rub the velvet petals between my fingers, but soon realized it wasn't a home, but a shop, the window displaying unusual shoes. Some looked as if they were made from seed pods, others were stitched from moss. I was captivated by a pair that appeared to be made from petals plucked from the walls.

This was a faery high street, seemingly catering for the most fortunate. Every element was designed to enhance the buyer's experience. I could imagine how busy it would be when the shops were open, the frisson of excitement as faeries acquired exquisite trinkets. I strolled past, admiring the temptations in every shop window, but then the strangest thing happened. Though the buildings were utterly beguiling, as I turned away and saw them from the corner of my eye, they appeared entirely different, nothing more than stone ruins overrun by ivy. When I looked back to check, all was as before, bewitching and magical.

Perhaps because of my awareness of the glamour responsible for the deceptive beauty, whatever enchantment had been cast over this part of the town suddenly lost its hold on me and I hurried on, keen to leave.

Despite my best intentions, however, I was irresistibly drawn to a window filled with mirrors.

They came in every shape and size, from shards to full length, round to diamond, and everything in between. None of them reflected my face or the street behind me.

One showed a Victorian horse and carriage trundling past a castle on a rainy day, another two women in Regency silks sipping tea in a small lounge. There was an empty room in an immaculate Tudor house, the face of a smiling child, the silhouette of skeletal branches against an indigo sky.

Confused by the differing images, my gaze traveled swiftly across them, until I saw something that made my heart stop.

"Grandma?"

She was sitting up in bed looking healthier than I had seen her in years. Around her wrist was an unfamiliar bracelet, spun from plain yarn. I wondered where it had come from.

"Grandma!" I called again, my palms pressed against the glass, wondering — hoping — she could hear me. But the voice which answered wasn't hers.

"Are you well?"

I spun to see two women approaching me. One was tall and elegant, chestnut hair gleaming against her brown skin, her dress the color of foxgloves. From her fluid movement and her catlike features, I knew she was a faery. Her companion wore a gown as golden as the hair which cascaded in ringlets down her back, and was undeniably human.

They looked like two figures from a history book, promenading in gowns that were a mismatch of styles: a frilly ruff at their throats, but a low empire neckline; puffy capped sleeves and a loose muslin bodice; a full skirt upon many petticoats, with a bustle at the back. Each carried a parasol, though the light remained a soft rose gold.

Apart from them the town remained deserted.

Realizing I hadn't answered, I blinked and found my voice. "Um, yes, I just saw someone I knew in the mirror."

The human nodded sympathetically. "Someone who's dead?"

"What? No!"

The faery tilted her head. "You do not understand the mirrors," she surmised. "Some show what is, others what has been, a few what is to come. There are those that reveal memories, dreams, desires. Some reflect your fears, though I don't believe they are much in demand."

I glanced back at the shop window, where all the images had changed, and wondered whether Grandma had been a reflection of my hope, or a glimpse of what awaited me when my tasks were complete. Perhaps it was merely another faery trick designed to wrong-foot me.

"I like your dress," the human said.

"Yes, it's unusual," the faery added, with a disdainful smile.

"I made it," I said, conscious of what a mess I must look compared to them. "I haven't been here long."

"You're new?" The human was delighted. "Oh, Lassila, she's only just arrived!"

The faery raised a perfectly groomed brow. "I would never have guessed."

"I'm Marigold," the human said, offering me her hand, which I thought she meant to shake but instead she brushed her palm against mine, as if she didn't really understand the gesture. "I should have known you hadn't been here long, we never see anybody else out this early. The shops don't open for a few more hours."

"That's okay," I said. "I'm passing through. I have another errand to run."

"Walking alone? You consider that safe?" Lassila's question sounded more like a threat and our eyes locked in mutual dislike.

"Yes, you should come and visit us tomorrow," Marigold said, either oblivious to the tension, or ignoring it. "We can tell you everything you need to know to be content here." She delved into her little shoulder bag and extracted a small twig, which she held out to me. "Snap that when you set off and follow the trail. It'll bring you to us."

I had no idea what that meant, but tucked the twig into my pocket with a nod of thanks.

"It'll be delightful to hear about home," Marigold said, with a girlish giggle. "Won't it, Lassila?"

"I can hardly contain my excitement," the faery replied, but Marigold didn't seem to notice her sarcasm.

"Until tomorrow then," Marigold said, sliding her arm through Lassila's and turning to walk back through the town.

For a moment, I watched them, feeling disconcerted. So far I had met almost as many humans here as faeries. Unlike Conor though, Marigold hadn't appeared to be a servant. While the prospect of seeing them again made me anxious, I suspected Marigold might reveal more about this place than Conor. Anything I could learn might help me get home sooner.

The image of Grandma in the strange mirror was imprinted on my mind, as I continued along the road with renewed determination. I left the shops behind, the hedgerows reappearing, the cobbles thinning until I was on a dirt path once more. The longer I walked, the more I began to doubt what Conor had said.

The sun was sinking in the sky, giving way to the rise of the two moons, when I saw the fork in the road, the trees looming black against the oncoming violet.

My eyes quickly adjusted to the gloom and I took the path, which was no more than flattened grass almost hidden beneath the overgrown hedges. It had taken most of the day to reach the forest, but certainly hadn't felt more than a few hours. A day didn't seem to be the same length here, a reminder that I'd be wise not to make any assumptions.

Barely any light penetrated the canopy of the trees, but I relished the calm of the near-darkness. The smell of damp earth soothed me and I filled my lungs with fresh forest air. That was when I heard it. The trill of a wren. The laughing call of the green woodpecker. The liquid song of a blackbird. Soon birdsong surrounded me and though hearing it at night was peculiar, it was a relief to know it existed. My spirits lifted.

I could do this. All I needed was to find some nettles, fill the sack, and complete my first task. Simple.

The path twisted and turned, forking in different directions. I always took the right turn, so that it would be easy to find my way back, scanning the woodland for my quarry as I went.

After a while, I spotted a dense patch of nettles, but reaching them would mean diverting deeper into the trees. I hesitated. Leaving the path was never a good idea in any of the stories Grandma had told me. Often those who strayed never found their way back again. Given that I was already deep in a faery forest, perhaps it was too late for such concerns. Besides, it wasn't far, I could keep the path within sight and not get lost.

I'd only taken a couple of steps into the undergrowth, when someone grabbed my arm, pulling me backwards. We tumbled to the ground and I gaped in horror as a writhing tangle of thorny vines sprang up to encircle the spot where I'd been standing moments before. I would have been caught in that terrible trap, were it not for . . .

I turned to see who I should thank for saving me and frowned in confusion.

"Conor?"

# Five

y gratitude evaporated instantly as I scrambled away from him. "What are you doing here?"

"Saving your life," he replied, visibly puzzled as he reached for the lantern I'd knocked from his hand. "Would you rather I hadn't?"

Glancing again at the thorny trap that would have devoured me, I knew he was right. But that only made me more suspicious of him.

"Did you follow me?"

"Obviously," he said. "You're welcome."

I rounded on him in fury. "First you were unfriendly. Then you spy on me, and you want me to thank you? What's your problem?"

To his credit, Conor looked ashamed. "I'm sorry. I was rude earlier. You caught me off guard, I'm not used to company. It's been just me and Morcan for a long time and he doesn't say a lot. I thought perhaps he was replacing me. It's not an excuse for my behavior, but you're new and then you wandered off and I was worried something might happen to you. So I came to check you were all right. I really am sorry."

He seemed genuine and I relented. "Apology accepted. You don't have anything to feel guilty about, so you can go back now."

Conor frowned. "You're not coming?"

"No, I have to complete my task."

"That's why you're here?" He sounded worried.

"Why else would I be wandering around a woodland at nighttime?" I asked.

"I thought you were trying to run away."

Was it strange that I hadn't even considered that option? But why would I jeopardise my deal to save Grandma in such a way?

"Is that what you did when you came here?" I asked. "Tried to run?"

His blue eyes shone almost purple in the red moonlight. "It's what everyone does."

I heard the challenge in his words and held his gaze. "Well, not me. Now, if you'll excuse me, I need to get on."

"It's not safe here," Conor warned. "That trap? One of many. This place is dangerous, Nettle. Like nothing you've ever known before."

"I don't have a choice." Why couldn't he understand that?

"Then come back in the sunlight, at least. You'll stand a better chance of surviving."

"I can't! I have to do this at night, it's part of the deal."

Conor studied my face for a while, and I thought he was going to tell me I was stupid, or wish me good luck and leave, but instead, he sighed. "What exactly did Ellion tell you to do?"

I held up the sack. "Fill this with nettles, gathered from this woodland under the light of the two moons."

"Then let me help you. Before you get yourself killed."

I raised my eyebrows. "You? Want to help me? I thought you said our tasks were impossible."

"They are," he said. "It sounds simple enough, nevertheless I guarantee there will be some faery mischief about it. But I can't leave you wandering around on your own when you don't know what you're dealing with."

"I'm sure I can cope," I said. "Come if you want, I can't stop you from being here."

Conor laughed, an unexpected sound that took us equally by surprise. "You're too kind."

We were teetering on the boundary between enmity and friendship, both equally uncertain. Neither of us was natural at being sociable, neither of us knew whether we could trust the other. Then he offered me a slight smile, and I returned it. An unspoken truce that we would start again with this uneasy alliance.

Without a word, we walked along the path. I hoped we would find some nettles where I could reach them without risking more death traps and, though I hated to admit it, I was glad to have some company.

"You know, you're lucky I came after you," Conor said after a while, a hint of humor in his voice.

"Why's that?" I asked.

"Because even if that trap hadn't got you, you'd never have found your way out of the forest again."

"I'll have you know I had made a mental map of the route I'd taken," I said, mildly indignant.

"Wouldn't have mattered," he replied. "These are faery paths. They shift and change as frequently as the wind, if you don't have something to protect you from the magic." He held up his wrist, revealing three bands of shimmering thread, and pointed to a sage green one. "This will make sure we find the way back, rather than spend the rest of our days searching for an exit."

"Where did you get that?"

"From the night market. We can go there later if you want. You'll need your own if you're planning to make this a habit."

"Once I've got these nettles, I don't intend to come back," I said firmly.

"Whatever you say," he replied, but I heard the doubt in his voice.

We trailed along in uncomfortable silence until my curiosity outweighed my nerves.

"So what are the traps for? I assume not just to catch runaway humans?"

Conor gave me a sideways glance. "No, and trust me, getting caught in one wouldn't offer an escape worth having. They're set by Gizler, the goblin, who has the most horrifying shop you never want to see."

I waited for him to expand, but he didn't. "Okay, you can't casually mention a scary shop run by a goblin named Gizler and not expect me to have questions."

Conor laughed. "I've never been there, but I've been warned about it."

"Who by?"

"Morcan. He's the faery in charge of the stables, my boss. He's told me enough over the years to keep me alive."

"He must like you," I said.

Conor shook his head. "The faeries don't like us, Nettle. They are not our friends, no matter how convincing they may seem. Some, like the king, despise us but at least you know where you are with him. There are others whose interest in humans seems harmless, but isn't. At best, we're lapdogs to them. Disposable and replaceable. If you want my advice, keep your head down, work hard, and trust no one."

Silence fell between us again. "Sounds lonely," I said at last, understanding him a little more.

"It is."

His response did not invite further conversation and so I focused on my purpose for being here, scanning for nettles and only seeing them tantalizingly out of reach, off the safety of the path.

"How long *have* you been here?" He hadn't answered me before, but perhaps the thaw between us would change that. If not, I knew Conor would have no trouble telling me to mind my own business and I would let it go.

At first, I thought he was going to ignore me, but then he said, "Time is strange here. Sometimes it drags, then passes in a rush. Days are shorter, nights are longer, at least compared to what I remember. But sometimes I don't know whether I remember at all. Are they memories or simply dreams I cling to?"

"What *do* you remember?" I asked softly.

"The sky was different. Sometimes blue, more often grey. Rain, plenty of that." His brow furrowed as he thought. "Lush green fields that swiftly turned to mud. A coldness that reached my bones. Horses." He paused. "My mam." His sadness was palpable. "It's been a long time."

"You lived on a farm?"

He considered this. "I don't think it was ours. My da worked the land. I helped sometimes." Each new memory seemed to unlock another, and I kept silent, allowing him to work through them. "I fed the pig."

I tried to piece the fragments of his life together. He'd lived rurally, simply. That didn't necessarily mean it had been too long ago. I'd need more details to work out when he'd come here. "Do you remember any books that you may have read?"

The blank look on his face answered that.

"Who was the king? Or queen?"

"George," he said after a moment's recollection. "King George."

"Which one?"

He gave me a strange look. "The only one there's been."

My heart began to race. King George the *first*? History wasn't my strongest subject, but I knew my kings and queens well enough. That would mean Conor had been here since the early eighteenth century. More than three hundred years? I'd assumed it had been decades at most, and panic threatened to break me. I couldn't be here that long. I couldn't.

"A lot of time has passed," I said, trying to keep my voice steady.

He nodded as if this was hardly a revelation. "I aged to begin with," he said. "Then it slowed down and I have remained the same for countless turns of the moons. Fit and healthy to perform my service to the king. To be here is to gain an unnaturally long life and, believe me, that isn't the gift you might expect. That's why I made the deal with Locryn. I wasn't thinking clearly in my desperation to go home and all I managed to do was deepen my ties to this realm."

His misery made me want to offer some morsel of comfort, yet what could I possibly say? I wished I'd heeded the warning in his first response and left it alone. My own situation seemed more precarious than ever.

"Look!" I pointed to a huge bed of nettles flanking the path, relieved to be distracted from the bleakness of our conversation. "These will do very nicely," I said, running gratefully toward them. I'd been starting to worry we wouldn't find any.

As I pulled out the knife Ellion had given me, Conor held the lantern up to illuminate the plants. "Don't you need gloves?"

I shook my head. "Nettles have never stung me."

"Hence the name?"

"Something like that," I said, as I somewhat self-consciously slid my hand down the stems. They weren't quite the same as nettles at home, which shouldn't have been a surprise. The stems were thicker, coarser, and shimmered as if they'd been dipped in glitter. The leaves were similar, but with a deadly serrated edge. One wrong move and they'd easily slice through flesh. I would have to be careful—a lifetime of being impervious to the effect of nettles' venom had left me dangerously casual about the risk they posed here. And while they were all definitely stinging nettles, they were covered in the delicate white flowers I'd only ever seen on dead nettles before.

Holding several stems in my fist, I took the knife to make the first cut. The blade bounced off them, not making a dent. Interesting. When I tried again, the knife remained ineffective.

I peered at Conor, who looked as confused as I was.

"Is it blunt?" he asked.

Cautiously, I touched the knife against my finger and as red blood blossomed, I winced. "No, it's like a razor. Why won't it cut through the nettles?"

"Try the leaves?"

I took his advice, but it was like attempting to slice iron with rubber.

Not willing to accept defeat, I tried as many different ways as possible – one stem, high up, low down, bending the stems together. Nothing worked.

"Told you," Conor said. "It's an impossible task."

"No!" I shouted, refusing to believe it. "No, no, no." I hacked pointlessly at the nettles with my useless knife before, exhausted, I collapsed to the ground.

"I'm sorry." Conor sounded genuinely disappointed for me. "I know how much you wanted to believe it was possible."

"Why?" I hated the despair in my voice. "Why would the king ask us to do things he knows we can't accomplish? Does he just want to mock us?"

"I suppose he doesn't want us to leave," Conor said, kneeling in front of me. "Maybe it amuses him to watch us struggle. Who knows?"

"There must be some reason behind it. Why nettles? Why would he want me to cut them down?"

Conor shrugged. "He's a faery, I don't think there has to be a reason. Perhaps because of your name?"

Something was tugging at my memory. "At home, Grandma always said that nettles marked the threshold between our two worlds. The fact that I fell through them supports that."

"You came here through nettles?" Conor was trying to make sense of my garbled words.

Ignoring his question, I tapped the bone blade against the ground. "What if they have some sort of magical property? Something protective. Something that would prevent this knife destroying them." I looked at Conor. "Do you know whether the faeries fear nettles?"

Conor shook his head. "Truthfully, before you appeared, I can't remember the last time I even heard the word nettle. From what I've heard them say, the only thing faeries fear is the metal in our world which is why they have none here—"

"That's it!" I cut him off.

"What?" he asked, while I reached into my deep pocket.

"This!" I pulled out my penknife victoriously. "In all the stories my grandma ever told me, iron was the only thing that could harm the faeries, so I think you're right. These nettles have some sort of enchantment about them, certainly faery weapons are useless against them. But what if my knife isn't? Ellion never specified I had to use the knife he gave me. The only rules were to fill the bag with cut nettles beneath the two moons."

Excited, I grasped a handful of nettles once more and pressed my penknife to the stems. The blade glided through with ease, and I cried out in delight.

"It worked!"

"So it did," Conor agreed, shaking his head in disbelief.

"Ha! Take that, Locryn!" I shouted to the treetops, causing Conor to gesture at me to shut up.

"Don't gloat, just get on with it. The sooner you fill that bag, the sooner we can get out of here." I could hear the admiration in his voice that I'd succeeded though.

I worked quickly and efficiently, cutting the stems low down to get as much of the plant as possible into the sack, while leaving enough to be able to grow back, taking care of the treacherous leaves as I threw them in.

"You really came through nettles?" Conor asked, as he watched me chopping away.

"Yeah, and I landed somewhere completely different before the Night Riders caught me. They thought I was a spy, which is ridiculous."

"The Night Riders?" Conor whistled. "They probably thought you worked for the queen."

"Are the king and queen rivals?" I asked. "Because I was practically accused of treason when they thought I was spying for her."

"Rivals, lovers, enemies. They're married, but their union has always been tempestuous. They're in love one minute, at war the next. They separated a while ago, over an argument so old, no one remembers what happened. Only that the moorland and forest kingdoms are no longer joined in any kind of peace."

I frowned. "Aren't we in the forest?"

"We're in *a* forest. Not *the* forest. The moorland has woodlands, but they're not part of the queen's forest court. No, to stray into her court would be considered treason."

"By the king or the queen?"

"Both." He shivered involuntarily. "Maybe we shouldn't talk about this here. Who knows what might be listening."

His wariness was enough to dissuade me from inquiring quite what he meant. Instead, I worked faster cutting the nettles, wanting to be done, the patch growing ever smaller.

"That must be enough," I said, as I cut the last of the crop. "Hopefully we won't need to find another patch."

I stepped to the sack to add my final handful, and any sense of triumph vanished. I didn't want to believe what I was seeing, but there was no denying it.

The sack was empty.

# SIX

"No!" I cried, as I reached into the bag for nettles that clearly weren't there. "Where are they?"

Conor joined me as I put the last stems in, and we watched as they fell into the sack and disappeared before our eyes.

"They enchanted the sack too?" I wasn't despairing anymore, I was furious. "That's cheating!"

To his credit, Conor didn't say he'd told me so. He rested a hand on my shoulder. "We should go," he said. "There's nothing more you can do."

I glared at him. "That's it? I simply resign myself to my grandma dying?"

"That was the deal you made?"

I nodded. "My whole life my grandma warned me about the faeries, told me all the tales. And first chance I had I made a deal with them. Three tasks. I can't even complete one."

Conor couldn't hide his shock. "You agreed to *three*?"

Tears sprang to my eyes. "I couldn't bear for her to die," I whispered. "I didn't want to be left alone."

"I'm sorry," Conor said, and it sounded as though he meant it. "Come on, there isn't much moonlight left. We need to go."

After tucking my penknife safely back into my pocket and gathering up the empty sack, I allowed Conor to guide me along the woodland path.

I observed the threads wrapped around his wrist that kept us safe from any more trickery. I was going to need some after all. Because although I had fallen at the first hurdle, I wasn't ready to give up. I couldn't. I had to save Grandma. It didn't matter that the game was heavily weighted in Locryn's favor, or that the odds were infinitesimal. The alternative was to accept my fate. Besides I'd only been here a day and already I'd overcome the problem of the useless knife. In time, I'd find a way to resolve the sack issue. Even if I spent the rest of my life trying, that was better than spending it defeated.

The walk back to the town seemed quicker than I remembered and when I mentioned it to Conor, he gestured to the gold thread on his wrist. "This enchantment allows you to travel along a faery road faster."

I glanced up at him. "For someone who hates the faeries so much and claims not to trust them, you use a lot of their magic."

"Only what helps me survive," he said shortly. "This," he touched the thread, glimmering scarlet, "symbolises my status as a servant to the king. That offers its own protection when I'm in the market."

"Can we go there now?" I asked. "I think I might need some help of my own."

Conor nodded. "Be careful though," he warned. "The sellers have everything imaginable and humans are easy targets. You'll be offered charms, enchantments, things to make you prettier, taller, stop your hair growing, or make it grow depending on which they think you need. They want you to look pleasing to their eyes, to their very narrow definition of beauty."

"I don't imagine there's an enchantment strong enough to make my hair behave," I joked, trying to ease my nerves.

"Don't eat food there either," Conor continued, remaining serious. "I'll find you some at the palace. All of it binds us to this world more tightly, but you'll have to eat something, and you don't want to risk the market food." He paused before adding, "I like your hair the way it is."

Before I had time to register the compliment, the sound of the marketplace reached my ears and my stomach clenched.

Conor hadn't made it sound the safest place, and I'd already experienced the strange bewitchment of the other shops, but I couldn't deny the curiosity that stirred within me.

As the stalls appeared in the distance, so did the crowds. Taking a deep breath, I skipped into a run to keep up with Conor's long stride. He didn't want to be here any longer than necessary.

It was like nothing I'd ever seen. So many faeries. Some in finery, others more modestly dressed. Some were identifiable purely by their poise and grace, others were unmissable because of the wings on their backs.

Conor grabbed my arm. "Don't gawp, it's rude."

He was right, of course, but I couldn't stop gazing at the gauzelike wings all around me. There weren't many humans, but I spotted a few. Some walked arm in arm with faeries. Others trailed miserably behind, carrying the goods of their faery masters. And none looked old, although I knew from Conor that appearances here were deceptive.

Then there were the others who seemed neither faery nor human. They had none of the faeries' flawless beauty, but still possessed an otherworldly quality. I wanted to ask Conor about them, but the market was noisy. The bartering battled against music which sought to claim me as much now as the first time I'd heard it, flung over the back of a Night Rider's horse. Every impulse I had compelled me to dance to its bewitching beat and I had to concentrate on the back of Conor's head to ground myself.

"Want a potion?" a seller called to me, as I glanced at his stall. The faery was offering me a dazzling smile, and I couldn't help but drift toward him. "I have every kind," he purred. "Something to soften your dreams? Or to poison someone else's?" Reading my expression, he changed tack. "Ah, I see what you're after. Something to single you out—an extra thumb perhaps?"

Conor appeared at my side, holding his wrist up so that the faery could see his red thread. "She's with me."

The faery nodded, acknowledging that while I was in Conor's company I was off-limits, but he grinned at me anyway. "Come and see me again. I'm sure I can find something to tempt you with."

I muttered half-hearted thanks and allowed Conor to pull me away.

"Stay close," he said. "Gammi's stall is just over here."

We hadn't walked far when a voice bellowed, "Conor!"

I'd expected the owner of such a voice to be a giant, but the stall-holder was half my height, with three braids of silver hair sprouting from an otherwise bald head. Her skin sparkled, her face rounder than the faeries'. Between thin lips were teeth like jagged stone and I knew not to underestimate this woman, no matter how small she was. Her stall was covered in threads of every texture and color, some neatly rolled on spindles, others in a messy tangle.

"Hi, Gammi," Conor greeted her. "Good night so far?"

"All the better for seeing you. What do you need?"

"Actually, my friend here is your customer tonight." He pushed me slightly forward to stand fully under Gammi's scrutiny.

"Fresh meat?" The stall-holder leaped onto her table to stand right in front of me, drinking me in like a glass of water in the desert. She placed a bony finger on my chin, pulling my face up and down as she inspected me and apparently found me lacking, because a frown creased her lined forehead. "You smell different," she said, in a somewhat accusatory manner.

I had no idea what to say to that, so tried to focus on why we were here. "I'm wondering if I could have some of the same thread as Conor?"

Gammi glanced at Conor, who held up his wrist. "She needs not to get lost in the woods."

"Marvelous!" Gammi cried, clapping her hands before rummaging on the table. "No, that's not it, no, no," she muttered as she rifled through her wares, before finding what she was looking for and holding it up triumphantly.

"Gammi's finest thread. No one's going to be lost anywhere with this beauty."

"Thank you," I said. "How much is it?" And as soon as I asked the question I realized I might not like the answer. Grandma's stories had suggested it wouldn't be as simple as exchanging coins for goods here.

"Hmm." Gammi considered this. "How about a tooth?"

"What?" I glanced anxiously at Conor who said nothing.

"From the back, you'll never notice," Gammi said, beaming.

"Is there anything else you'd accept?" I ventured.

"How about your secret?" she said, flashing her own teeth at me.

"What secret?"

"The one that clings to you like a burr," she said. "The one that makes you oh so interesting."

I shook my head apologetically. "I've no idea what you're talking about."

Gammi looked disappointed. "A tooth it is then."

As panic gripped, a thought occurred to me. Grandma and I had left delicious treats out as gifts for the faeries for years, mindful of the stories that told of their love of human food. It was time to find out how true they were.

"Who wants a boring old tooth," I said, "when you could have this?" And I pulled a lemon sherbet from my pocket as if it was a nugget of gold.

Gammi gasped and reached for it.

I snatched it back. "Uh uh, not so fast," I said, as if I held the most valuable thing on earth. "I can't just give this away."

"What is it?" Gammi asked, her eyes wide with excitement.

"A sherbet," I said in my most tempting voice.

"A sherbet?" She breathed the word. "Let's trade. That for the thread." She hopped from leg to leg, unable to contain her eagerness.

"I don't know," I said coyly, "I'm not sure it's worth it."

I didn't expect to achieve anything beyond trying not to seem like a total pushover, but to my surprise, she snatched up a length of the gold thread that Conor wore.

"Take this too, so you can move more swiftly about the realm. Now hand it over."

"It's a deal," I said, holding out the sherbet, which she snatched greedily as she flung the threads at me.

She held it up to the crimson moon, the red light glowing on the wrapper, which she peeled off in wonder, crinkling it in her hand. The sound amused her and she cackled loudly, scrunching it over and over.

"The wrapper isn't even the best part," I said, pointing to the candy. "Pop that in your mouth and—"

Before I could advise her to suck it, Gammi had thrown it between her stony teeth and crunched. As the sherbet fizzed on her tongue, her eyes practically bulged out of her head and she howled with delight.

It was enough to catch the attention of those around us and Conor suddenly tugged my arm.

"We should go," he said. "They're all going to want one now."

I smiled, but quickly realized he wasn't sharing my amusement. In fact, he looked downright scared.

So I nodded and we hurried away from Gammi's stall and the crowd gathering there.

"You have food from the human world?" Conor hissed. "Foolish to offer that to a hobgoblin. You're lucky that Gammi is trustworthy."

So that's what all the non-faery, non-human beings were, hobgoblins. There were certainly a lot of them in the market, some selling, others buying, and I'd spotted an elegant couple striding through the street dressed in ostentatious finery.

"So if Gammi is a hobgoblin, what do goblins look like?" I asked, sensing it was wise to learn how things worked here as fast as possible.

"You're unlikely to see goblins this close to the palace," Conor replied. "They tend to keep their distance from the faeries. Locryn likes goblins as much as he likes humans, and the feeling is mutual." He paused. "Do you have more of whatever you gave Gammi?"

"Yes, do you want one?"

A shadow fell across his face. "I haven't eaten anything from home for a long time."

"I don't think you'll ever have tasted something like candy," I said.

He was tempted, I could tell, but in the end, he shook his head. "No, thank you. Keep them secret. Food from the human world is practically worshipped here and there are plenty who would have no problem taking what they want from you."

We made our way through the archway in the palace wall and down the overgrown path toward the stables. As we walked, I tied the threads around my wrist, flinching at the hot prickle as they rested against my skin.

"It's the spell binding to you," Conor explained as I rubbed at it. "The sensation will fade."

Seconds later he was proved right, and I sighed with relief.

When we reached the yard, Conor turned to me uncertainly. "What did Gammi mean about you having a secret?"

"I have no idea," I answered honestly. "What you see is what you get. Maybe it was the nettles' magic lingering on my dress or something?"

"Maybe." Conor stared at me for a moment and then reached forward. I flinched slightly, but he simply removed a strand of straw from my hair. "Get some sleep," he said and then walked away, leaving me with a heart that beat too fast.

I retreated into my dark stable, searching blindly for the pile of straw and collapsing onto it. The night might not have gone as I'd hoped, with my task far from complete, but I had the threads. Now I could safely return to the forest tomorrow and every night afterwards, until I found a way to complete my mission.

*Don't worry, Grandma*, I thought, as sleep stole me away. *I will save you. No matter what.*

# SEVEN

When the sun next rose, I found myself weaving through a narrow alleyway as I followed a wisp of golden mist and wondered whether I was still dreaming.

I hadn't slept brilliantly on the unforgivingly hard floor, the straw offering little comfort or warmth, but I'd dozed for a while before I'd heard the Night Riders thunder in and leave their horses for Conor to look after.

I'd been uncertain whether to offer my assistance or not to interfere, and then remembered that Marigold had invited me to visit.

I'd dug the small twig that she'd given me out of my pocket, and, before I could change my mind, snapped it as she'd instructed.

Immediately the golden mist had appeared and the only reasonable thing to do had been to follow it.

It had led me through twisting, turning passageways in the town and along the narrow alley with towering stone walls, reaching a dead end with the most peculiar structure ahead of me. It looked as though several old trees had long ago leaned in for a group hug and never let go. The bark had been painted with windows and a door drawn on. It was outside this painted door that the wisp I'd followed disappeared.

I glanced about, and wondered far later than I should have whether this was a good idea. While Marigold had been friendly enough, she was a stranger and Lassila had been positively scary. With a reckless lack of caution, I knocked on the bark masquerading as a door.

Seconds later, a line glowed in the tree and a door that absolutely had not been there before swung open.

"Hello?" I called, listening to my voice echo. "May I come in?"

When no answer came, I stepped into the hallway, my curiosity overriding my trepidation. It was tall and spacious and should not have been possible within the structure I saw outside. Odder still was the mismatch of family portraits hanging from cracked walls and the ceramic vase upon a crooked table. Roots protruded from the ceiling, and on a branch that burst from the wall sat an owl, who watched me intently. I recoiled as my toes squelched in the sludge of rotting leaves that carpeted the floor, and I announced my presence once more.

A door to my right burst open and Marigold stared at me crossly. "You're late."

"I'm sorry."

"Never mind, you're here now." She gestured for me to join her in the room.

Lassila was there, sitting on a swing made of twisted vines by an ornate fireplace. It was a peculiar sight. Creeping roses ran up the walls as if on a trellis, but they were wilting, the petals curling at the edges and a faint scent of decomposing plants filled the air.

"Sit where you like," Lassila said with disinterest and not moving an inch. I could tell that beneath her façade she was far more curious about me than she was letting on.

"Thank you for inviting me," I said, opting for a square-armed chair with a high back, moss for a cushion, and ivy tangled through the polished wood frame. "You have a lovely home."

Marigold brought me a delicate porcelain cup, containing what looked—and smelled—like pond water.

"Here," she said proudly. "Just like you drink back home. Lassila has taught me about human ways."

I glanced at Lassila who fixed me with a challenging gaze. "Thank you," I said to Marigold, taking the vile concoction and bringing the cup to my lips. But I wasn't going to let a drop touch them.

"You must tell us your name," Lassila drawled.

"I'm Nettle."

# Nettle

"How peculiar," said Marigold. "I'm not sure I would like to be named after something so prickly and poisonous. And that gown you're wearing, it's the same as yesterday, is it not?"

I heard her disapproval and I looked down at my dirty dress. Painful memories resurfaced of how the girls in the village had shamed me for being different. I smoothed the linen and took a breath. "Yes. This is me." To my relief my tone was even, not betraying my emotions.

Marigold looked unconvinced. "For five memories, you can purchase some lovely cloth at the market," she hinted.

"Memories?" Somehow that seemed so much worse than a tooth.

"Not anything that matters," Marigold assured me, perhaps noting the horror on my face. "You won't miss them."

I didn't feel I knew her well enough to insist I would, that my memories of home, of Grandma, were the most precious things to me and what I was clinging to in order to survive here. And, more importantly, escape.

"Give her one of your old gowns," Lassila said, an offer that I suspected stemmed less from generosity and more from a desire to bring an end to the matter.

"What a wonderful idea," Marigold agreed.

A faery servant was summoned and quickly dispatched to fetch garments. Marigold resumed sipping her pond water and offered me a tiny layered cake.

Lassila noticed my hesitation and laughed. "We aren't trying to poison you."

"You mustn't worry," Marigold added. "Faery food isn't harmful to humans. I've been eating it all my life and am perfectly well as you can see."

There was something in the wickedness of Lassila's smile that made me doubt that statement. I accepted a cake nevertheless, with as much intention to eat it as drink the foul water.

"Perhaps you can explain why I've been here for over a day and am only now aware of my hunger," I asked, hoping I sounded more intrigued than afraid.

"You are in our realm now," Lassila said. "You cannot expect the rules to be the same."

"No, indeed." I couldn't help but think she wasn't just talking about food. "May I ask, Marigold, how you came to be here?"

"Oh yes, I was incredibly fortunate. You see my human mother had died and as a helpless babe, I would have soon joined her in the afterlife, but my faery father — Lord Lindelburr — saw me through one of his mirrors and came to rescue me."

"How kind of him." Again, I noticed Lassila's smirk and wondered whether fortune and kindness had played any part. "And how do you know each other? Are you related to Lord Lindelburr?" I asked Lassila.

"Lassila is another of his wards." Marigold jumped in to reply before Lassila had a chance. "Lord Lindelburr took her in too."

"What happened to your family?" I pressed Lassila. "I thought faeries were immortal?"

"Not quite, although I can see why your small mind might struggle to comprehend our longevity," she replied coldly. Whatever her story was, she didn't want to tell me. Which was her choice—I wasn't inclined to believe her anyway.

"How long have you been friends?" I wasn't sure how long Marigold had been here and hoped it hadn't been centuries like Conor.

Marigold opened her mouth to answer, but paused. "You know, I can't recall. It's been a long time, but I cannot even remember how we met!"

I glanced at Lassila, who didn't rush to remind her.

Marigold filled the awkward silence. "You're so lucky to have come to this place."

"Yes, tell us how that happened," Lassila asked, arching a perfect brow. "It is unusual for a human so old to be brought here."

Was she insulting my age? When she could be thousands of years old and I was barely brushing the threshold of adulthood? I didn't mind it when Grandma called me an old soul, but this was a bit rich.

"I wasn't brought here," I said. "It was simply an accident."

"You stumbled upon a portal?" Marigold asked, as if this was the most marvelous luck.

"More or less," I replied.

"Do you have a faery guardian? I'm sure Lord Lindelburr wouldn't mind you living here with us!"

Fortunately, Lassila prevented me from having to decline. "We do not have the room. I'm sure Nettle can flourish perfectly well on her own."

I returned a smile as genuine as her own, which was to say not at all. "I already have a position at the palace." A slight bending of the truth, but that seemed perfectly acceptable here.

"How wonderful!" Marigold was impressed.

Lassila, not so much. "I imagine from the straw clinging to every part of you that you are in the stables."

I briefly wondered what the equivalent of leaving her a toffee onion might be. "Yes, and very comfortable they are too," I said sweetly. "In fact, I must get back."

"Of course," Marigold said, rising to her feet. "Shall we see you at the ball the night after next?"

My blank expression gave her my answer.

"You don't know? Oh, Lassila, tell her!"

Lassila's eyes met mine as she said, "Every three moons there is a masquerade ball at the palace. While the king does not favor the humans who dwell in his realm, he accepts that many of his subjects feel more fondly toward the few among us. They are only permitted to attend the masquerades so that he isn't forced to look upon them."

"You must come!" Marigold exclaimed.

I had no intention of attending a ball. I wanted to spend every spare minute of the moonlight trying to work out how to cut those nettles and complete my first task. But I could also tell how much my presence would irritate Lassila, and the petty part of me won.

"I'd love to join you."

It was only after I'd left, with a parcel Marigold had pressed on me, complete with a twig to guide me home and another for next time, that I cursed myself. What had I been thinking? For the chance to annoy Lassila, I'd committed to wasting an entire night with her and a host of other faeries, including the king himself who could not have made his feelings about me clearer. A ball? So many faeries? How would I last five minutes?

The yard was empty when I returned, with no sign of Conor, so I went to my stable and unwrapped the parcel. Inside was a pretty white dress, simple and plain. I couldn't imagine Marigold ever wearing something with such clean lines. It was distinctly faery though, like something a lost princess would wear in Grandma's stories. It would fit me well enough, I decided, but it lacked something important.

And so with my penknife and sewing kit, I set about giving it pockets.

# EIGHT

The journey to the woodland was much quicker thanks to Gammi's threads. The road moved swiftly beneath my feet and I reached the trees before the moons rose.

I waited for them to catch up with me before I ventured into the forest, armed once again with my sack and penknife. Perhaps tonight would be the night.

I soon realized something was wrong. Though I had entered the forest at the same point and taken the exact same path as before, nothing was familiar about my surroundings. I tried retracing my steps, but before I knew it, I was in a very different part of the forest.

It was darker, gloomier, the atmosphere far from welcoming.

Even so, it took my breath away.

Ancient oaks surrounded me, their gnarled trunks clothed in thick vines and lichen. Contorted branches reached to me, either for help or in desperate accusation. The path ceased to exist—instead, granite boulders jutted from the forest floor, irregular in size and position. The velvety moss covering them glowed scarlet from the light of the blood-red moon, so the stones looked as if they'd been stained by sacrificial offerings.

The air was thick with magic, I could practically taste it and I knew that while this place was hauntingly beautiful, it was also undoubtedly dangerous. To continue seemed unwise—the sensible thing would be to try to find my way back. Yet I'd only been brought here because the path had shifted—something Gammi's thread was supposed to prevent. If it wasn't working then going back might make things worse. I'd been gone from Grandma too long already, I didn't have time to waste being safe.

The most obvious problem with this place was the lack of nettles. And without a path to follow, I'd have to risk traps and anything else that might be lurking in the woods.

"You'll just have to be careful then, won't you?" I said, speaking out loud as I often did at home. In the absence of others, you become your own greatest friend.

Slowly, I climbed onto the first boulder, savoring the softness of the moss between my toes. Nature had always been magical to me, but here it literally was. For a moment, I didn't move, just breathed in the atmosphere. It sharpened my wits. There was a path of sorts, across the boulders, I hadn't been able to see it before. The moss trailed in a wobbly line and that was what I followed, hopping from rock to rock, taking care not to get caught on the bony fingers of the oak branches.

*Nettle.*

The voice was faint on the wind, a welcome companion in such unnerving surroundings, and I strained to hear which direction it was coming from.

To my disappointment, I realized the sound echoed from the darkness of the trees. I peered into the shadows and an icy chill passed over me. Venturing into the unknown seemed a bad idea, but maybe it was the suggested route that was actually not to be trusted. In fact, the more I considered this, the more I wondered if it was signaled too obviously, as if the wood wanted me to take it. Could it be a way to lure me to my death?

My head hurt. Had I really convinced myself to deviate into the deep, dark woods because that was somehow safer than the path?

"I hope you're on my side," I said. Though I doubted whoever the voice belonged to could hear me, I needed someone to blame if this all went wrong. I changed course and hopped down from the boulders to stride into the inky darkness between the trees.

The difference hit me immediately. Peace. Calm. A nightingale's sweet song. The twisted branches no longer clawed, but ushered me gently along my way. My eyes adjusted to the barely-there moonlight, and I took in my surroundings. There was nothing but trees. Trees as far as the eye could see. Knotted and knobbly, tall and tangled, like a sprawling family that had grown out of hand over eternity. I rested my hand gently on the bark of the nearest and listened to the deep hum that emanated from it. These trees were not my enemies. Nor were they entirely my friends, but they would let me pass, I felt sure of it. As long as I did nothing to anger them.

"I only want to find some nettles," I promised them. "I won't take more than I need, they'll grow back quickly."

A rustling sound made me look down, and to my astonishment, dozens of leaves floated from the fallen piles around the tree trunks. Moving in a swirling formation, they surrounded me, before flying off like a russet kite. I hurried after them.

The earth was rough beneath my feet, but I had a sense of kinship with this woodland that allowed the first hint of happiness I'd experienced in a long time. Since before Grandma became ill.

I was captivated by the wonder of the flying leaves and as they swept me along through the labyrinth of trees, two broke away, fluttering back toward me.

I held out my hand, and as they landed there, I was startled to see that they were tiny sprites whose wings were as fragile as dried autumn leaves. They watched my open-mouthed surprise and whispered to each other behind their teeny hands.

"Hello," I said, wanting to be polite to these ethereal beings. "I'm Nettle."

One nodded respectfully to me, and before I could say anything else, they whirled swiftly back to join the others.

"Wait for me!" I called, not wanting to lose sight of them in the gloom. I had to run fast to keep up, and then came to an abrupt halt.

They'd led me to a glade, where they dispersed, and I was left to stare at the sight before me.

The clearing was circular, bordered by the twisted trees, and empty save for a single figure.

The faery had his back to me, so I saw his wings in all their stunning beauty. As delicate as skeleton leaves, they looked as if they were made from shadow. For all their apparent fragility, I could sense their strength too. They grew from his shoulder blades, and there wasn't an ounce of fat on his bare torso, his brown skin glittering as Locryn's had. His pants were entirely black, lacking any of the adornment the other faeries seemed to desire, and his black, silver-laced hair was loose and unkempt.

Much as his wings had captivated me, it was the fact that several of the trees had their branches encircling him in a strange embrace, that intrigued me the most.

I could hear them humming, both faery and trees in a peculiar communion. Though I knew I'd stumbled into something private, I couldn't look away.

Then the trees rustled and the faery turned his head in my direction.

It was Ellion.

At his gesture, the trees withdrew and the faery faced me with an impenetrable expression.

"I'm sorry," I said. "I didn't mean to intrude."

He ignored my apology. "What are you doing here?"

The severity of his voice unnerved me. I held up the sack. "Searching for nettles."

He glanced pointedly around. "As you can see, there are none."

"No." I wasn't sure what to say. "I'm just passing through."

Head down, I began to walk toward the other side of the clearing, but to my dismay, he wasn't finished with our conversation. He grabbed my arm, his eyes briefly falling on the threads tied at my wrist.

"How did you get here?" There was no doubt of the accusation in his tone.

"The paths kept shifting," I said. "If you ask me, this charm is completely faulty. I was surrounded by oaks and granite stones and then . . ." I paused, not wanting to mention the voice, and he seized on my hesitation.

"And then . . . what?"

I knew that he would see through any deception, so I settled for part of the truth.

"I followed some flying leaves."

"The leaflings? Interesting. They don't usually help anyone." He watched me, perhaps hoping for some response, but I had none to give. "And the trees don't tend to allow anyone to walk among them in this place," he added.

"They let you," I said with a shrug.

"Indeed." There was weight to the word, as if I'd answered a riddle without knowing it.

The silence that fell between us was awkward and his gaze unnerving. Walking off would be rude, so I fumbled for something in the way of conversation.

"Your wings are beautiful," I said, regretting it the instant the words left my mouth. Perhaps commenting on a faery's wings was inappropriate. "Sorry, it's just you didn't have them last time I saw you."

"Of course I did," he replied. "We often hide them from humans, that's all."

"Why?"

"Because they stare."

Given how intensely he'd been looking at me, that seemed a bit hypocritical. I scrunched my toes into the cool earth and wished he'd bid me farewell so I could escape. But he didn't and the silence was unbearable, forcing me to speak against my better judgement.

"Did the trees have anything interesting to say?" I asked jokingly, expecting him to mock me.

"The trees always have interesting information to share," Ellion replied in all seriousness.

"You really were talking to them?"

"What else would I have been doing?"

We regarded each other with equal confusion.

"I mean, I talk to trees all the time," I said, not wanting to offend him again. "But I never hear a reply. How wonderful to speak their language."

Ellion frowned, as if uncertain whether he should divulge what he was about to, but then he said, "I'm a shadow faery. It's among the gifts we have."

I shook my head apologetically. "I'm sorry, I don't know much about the different types of faeries. Is a shadow faery just one who moves through shadows like you do?"

His wings flapped in an almost angry response. "Just?" He scoffed. "We are the rarest of all faeries. We are feared. Loners. Cursed."

"I don't understand—" I stuttered, as he stepped toward me.

"We are faeries not intended to survive the punishment we were dealt. A penance too high to pay." The light of the moon caught his eyes, so they glimmered a menacing red. "I was sent to the human world, an exchange for a mortal. I was supposed to die there. But I did not. Shadow faeries are changelings." He smiled wickedly. "Changelings who come back."

# NINE

My grandma had told me many stories about changelings. Most included trickster faeries swapping a changeling for a human baby, stealing the mortal away to their realm to raise as a servant while the remaining changeling child sickened and died. Others suggested the changelings chose to come into the human world, greedy for the food found there. In all of them, changelings were peculiar creatures that were considered strange to look at, weak and very much unwanted.

I stared at Ellion, at his exquisite beauty, and found it hard to believe what he was telling me.

"You're a changeling?"

"I was. Now I'm a shadow faery."

"You lived in the human world?" My awkwardness melted away in the face of curiosity. I wanted to know more, to delve beneath the surface of the tales I'd been raised on. "How did you survive?"

Ellion closed his eyes, as though my questions wearied him. "You talk too much."

"Well, don't taunt me with tantalizing information." A bubble of irritation burst within me. "Or did you simply hope to scare me?"

He blinked, as if my response had not been what he'd expected. Then he surprised me by saying, "What do you wish to know?"

Where should I possibly start?

"So it's true that faeries steal humans away to this world, that's not just a story?"

"How did you think there came to be others here?" He sounded scathing at my stupidity.

"Well, I wasn't switched with a changeling," I pointed out. "And I met a girl called Marigold who said she had been rescued by a faery from certain death."

Ellion gave a snort of contempt. "Marigold Lindelburr wasn't rescued."

"She was stolen by the faeries?"

Ellion nodded. "It's not been uncommon through the ages. Many have long been fascinated by humankind and sought them out for amusement. Locryn would prefer not to have humans here, but when he ruled with Keita by his side, she convinced him to allow the faeries to have their fun."

"Does Marigold have no idea? She seems happy."

"I doubt that girl has any idea who she is or, more to the point, what she is. Lassila has used so many glamours on her over the decades, she can't be more than a shell of what she once was."

"That's barbaric," I muttered. "Why would they take her and bring her here?"

With a shrug, Ellion said, "I do not know the family well, but I assume Lord Lindelburr wanted a child for his wife, and when she grew old enough, a companion."

"Lassila is Lady Lindelburr?" Oh, poor Marigold. She was nothing more than a fly tangled in a web of lies. "So if she wasn't rescued, a changeling was left in her place?"

Ellion nodded, his jaw tense.

"But who? Who are the changelings? Are they faeries who wish to experience the human world?"

"Some are, though most don't retain their faery memories," he said, and I noticed his voice grew strained. "Others . . . well, our lives last thousands of years and it can take its toll. Some older faeries wish for a release and choose to take a form that will quickly expire."

I remembered what he'd said about it being a punishment. "What did you do to become a changeling?" I asked softly, and as he hunched his wings high, I was suddenly horribly aware of how vulnerable I was.

His eyes burned like flames. "My past is no business of yours."

He held my gaze, and once again I couldn't look away. At first I thought it was from fear, but then I realized I simply didn't want to, as though he held me enthralled.

"What are you doing here?" he asked again, only this time the accusation was gone, his voice a whisper.

He was employing some sort of magic on me. I could feel an answer being coaxed from deep within, some secret he wished to possess, but I only had the truth to give him. "Nettles. That's all."

Ellion blinked slowly and I almost stumbled forward as he released me from whatever spell he'd cast. "Well, then. Don't let me keep you."

The abruptness to the end of our conversation left me temporarily dizzy, the air around me cooling as he stepped away.

As oxygen returned to my lungs, I gathered myself. Unable to do more than offer him a nod goodbye, I hurried through the clearing, painfully aware of him watching me leave.

Reaching the other side, I leaned against a tree shielded from Ellion's view, and caught my breath.

*What was that?* I wondered, trying to make sense of it. From his strange questioning to his unexpected sharing, all wrapped up in his hypnotic presence, I was completely discombobulated.

As my head cleared, I began to understand. Undoubtedly, it had been another of the faeries' tricks, another distraction to keep me from completing my task. I had to keep that front and center of my thoughts. Because Locryn did not wish to keep his deal, he would deploy any means at his disposal to prevent me from succeeding.

"They'll have to try harder than that," I muttered as I pushed forward to explore this new part of the forest.

To my relief, there was a discernible path, flanked by swathes of bracken, and the odds of finding nettles here seemed high.

Silently thanking the leaflings for guiding me, I walked briskly, knowing there weren't many hours of moonlight left.

It didn't take long. This part of the woodland was filled with huge clumps of nettles, and I wasted no time in cutting them and filling my cursed sack. The fact they disappeared was irrelevant to me. I would keep trying until eventually it worked.

As I went through the motions, there was nothing to stop my wandering thoughts of Grandma, Bracken, and Moss. I missed them so much. Then my mind settled on Conor and I wondered how he'd come to be here. Had he been stolen like Marigold? And then all I could think about was Ellion, the intensity of his burning gaze, the raw power in his magnificent wings.

When the birds went to roost, and the sky began to lighten, I picked up my totally empty sack and took a breath. This was the moment I'd been avoiding — would the forest allow me to leave? The thread certainly hadn't helped me, but perhaps the leaflings would guide me out if all else failed?

The path meandered as unexpectedly as it had on the way in, but it took me quickly to the edge of the woodland, and I breathed a thank you to the trees for allowing me to leave. A shiver ran through me when I wondered how long they would continue to do so.

I was dreaming of my bed of straw as I traipsed back into the yard, and the last thing I was expecting to see was Conor fast asleep outside my stable door.

I gently shook his shoulder and he woke with a start.

"What are you doing out here?" He looked at the door. "You're supposed to be in there."

I held up the sack. "I went back for more nettles," I said. "What are *you* doing out here?"

He ran his hand through his hair, looking embarrassed. "I was worried that word might have spread about your candy. Wanted to make sure you were all right."

This was the last thing I was expecting him to say. "What, you thought Gammi might come back for more?" I teased, before realizing he was serious.

"No, no one can enter the king's grounds without his express permission," Conor said as he stood up. "But you have something of value, Nettle. Round here, people will go to great lengths if they think there's some benefit to them. You need to be careful."

"Okay."

"I mean it," he said. "It's dangerous."

I thought of the way Ellion had loomed before me in the clearing and believed him.

"Listen, have you had food yet?"

The cake that had remained untouched on the saucer at Marigold's house came to my mind, and my stomach growled. "No."

"Come on, I was about to eat," he said. "I have plenty to share."

After dropping my empty sack in the stable, I followed Conor, a glow of warmth igniting in my chest. I liked him. I liked having a friend. And though it was hard to be sure — I'd made this mistake before — he seemed to like me too.

*Don't get attached.* The little voice in my head that had protected me since my ill-fated attempts at friendships in the past offered wise counsel. Every time I had made myself even the teensiest bit vulnerable toward another person, it had ended with me being mocked, humiliated, and confused.

Conor lived in a hayloft above the stables, and the ladder was both steep and wobbly. But a smile danced on my lips when I saw his home. Several bales formed a mattress with a blanket rolled up for a pillow and another to keep him warm. A bale to sit on. And a dish of food waiting on another that served as a table, alongside a jug.

"I'm sorry there's only one seat," he said, gesturing for me to take it while he settled on the floor. "I've never had a guest before."

"Well, I'm rarely invited to be anyone's guest, so thank you." I gave him a genuine smile.

There were two chunks of bread in the dish, along with some berries I didn't recognize and some mixed grains and leaves. Conor took a piece of the bread, scooped some of the grains up with it, and then passed me what was left. "Sorry," he apologized again. "Only one plate."

"Have you got enough?" I asked, worried he'd left far more than half.

"Plenty." He passed me the water jug. "It reminds me of home. There were always times of scarcity, so everyone shared and took care of each other."

"How old were you when you came here?" I asked. "You obviously weren't a baby taken in exchange for a changeling."

"No, I was like you, came through a portal. A pair of hawthorn trees. Can't remember exactly how old I was, but I only remember a few harsh winters."

"I'm sorry," I said.

Conor shrugged. "It was the first faery trick I fell for. Someone was calling for help." He paused. "It sounded like my mother. They copied her voice to dupe me. I still wonder how long she searched for me before she gave up hope."

There were no words of comfort I could offer, so I said nothing.

With a sigh, he cleared his throat. "I envy those other humans in town, those stolen who don't remember what they left behind. Not like us. We're here at the whim of faery mischief. They lured me through those trees and you through the nettles." He glanced up at me. "How did they trick you into the patch?"

A cold guilt crept over me. He had been brought here against his will, had left behind family and loved ones. How could I tell him that I had all but invited the faeries to steal me away?

"I heard bells."

He nodded sadly, and I hated myself for making him feel sorry for me. "Would you tell me about it? About home?"

"My history isn't amazing," I admitted. "I can tell you what I know, paint a picture of how things have changed since you were there."

"I'd like that. It's all that matters to me," he said. "Going home one day." The clatter of dozens of hooves in the yard made him sigh. "But not today, there's work to do. You finish your food, you're welcome to stay as long as you like."

"I'll come down and help you if you want," I said, and he gave me a warm grin.

"I'd like that."

As Conor disappeared down the ladder, my guilt only grew. Gammi had accused me of having a secret. Ellion seemed to be teasing one from within me.

I hadn't any secret to offer either of them. But having lied to Conor about how I got here, I did now.

# TEN

After I had devoured the warm bread and delicious grains, which tasted like nothing I'd ever had before, I made my way down to join Conor. It briefly occurred to me that I should be exhausted after being up all night, but if I was learning anything it was that nothing was normal here.

"Right, what can I do?" I asked him.

He gestured to the row of a dozen stables behind him. "They need mucking out."

I eyed the vast black horses that occupied them, remembering their impossible speed. "What about them?"

"Tie them up on the other block," Conor said, before looking at my feet in worry. "We really should fetch you some boots."

I wanted to tell him not to bother, that I did everything back home barefoot, including mucking out, but I didn't want him to think I was strange. So I didn't object when he wandered off in search of a pair, nor when he returned with boots at least three sizes too big for me.

"Here," he said, crouching to slip them on my feet.

"It's like a bad version of Cinderella," I joked, and he looked up at me, a frown creasing his face.

"That name . . . was that a story?" His mind was clearly racing, the thread of a memory tugged, and I realized he recalled something from his past.

"Yes," I said, squatting to be level with him. "A faery tale. Maybe you heard it when you were younger?" My general history might be shaky but here Grandma had taught me well. I'd absorbed everything she could tell me about the origins of faery tales far and wide and knew that Perrault's version of the tale was spreading through England at that time and more than likely Ireland too.

"A faery tale?" he echoed. "Like these faeries?"

"No, Cinderella's faery was kind and good. She helped a girl who fell in love with a prince to live happily ever after."

"Definitely not like this then."

His sorrow was almost tangible, and I rested my hand over his.

He managed a smile, before he cleared his throat and stood up. "Did Cinderella have such fashionable boots?"

With a laugh I replied, 'She should be so lucky. She was stuck with glass slippers, which couldn't have been at all practical."

"Why aren't you working, boy? And who is your companion?" A voice boomed across the yard, and I stood quickly as a faery strode toward us.

He was dressed like the Night Riders—leather pants, shirtless, of course, with long silver hair knotted in a bun. The word that sprang to my mind to describe him was burly.

"Let me do the talking," Conor muttered under his breath. "Morcan, Ellion has ordered that Nettle stays here. She's offered to help with the horses."

Morcan growled. "That shadow faery goes too far." He looked me up and down critically.

Though Conor had told me to be quiet, I had to offer some defense. "I had my own pony and a donkey." Stupid really, how could that possibly compare to the Night Riders' steeds? "I'm no stranger to hard work."

Morcan's eyes narrowed before he responded with a nod at Conor.

While there appeared to be a grudging respect between the faery and human, the imbalance of power was unquestionable. Morcan would tolerate Conor, so long as Conor did exactly as he was told.

I set to work straight away, hating how my feet flopped about in the giant boots. Conor passed me a rope head collar, and I approached the first stable.

The mountain of a horse looked down at me through its long forelock, its eyes like smoky quartz.

"That's Pym," Conor said, as he stroked the nose of what seemed to be an identical horse. I had no idea how he could tell them apart. "She can be nippy, so watch out."

"Noted," I said, unfazed. Moss had always been a bitey little fiend. "Did you name them?"

Conor nodded. "The Night Riders aren't the type for sentimentality," he said. "They ride them, nothing more. It's me who looks after them."

I glanced back at Pym. "No wonder you get snappy if your rider doesn't care," I said, slipping the rope over her head, having to stand on tiptoe to reach.

She replied with a practiced nip to my shoulder and I growled at her. "Okay, I get it, you're a mighty warrior mare and I'm an insignificant human, but if you want a nice thick bed of straw, you might try being nicer to me."

Pym bared her teeth, but didn't bite again, so I decided that meant she understood me, even if she didn't like it.

Leading her out was intimidating though, her gait long, her mane flowing. She was breathtaking. I ran my hand down her neck and across her withers, remembering when I had been captured and forced to lie across them. What would have happened if I'd made it to the forest? Would I have found the voice that called me? Would I be bound to the queen in her land, rather than the king in his?

"Nettle," Conor hissed and broke my musing. I followed his gaze to where Morcan was leaning against the wall, arms folded and glaring at me.

It was time to work.

---

"You stink of horse." Lassila made no effort to disguise her repulsion.

"I washed her as you instructed," her maid, Nyla, insisted. And she had—I'd been forced into what could only be described as a pond in the middle of a room, where Nyla had scrubbed me despite my protests.

"If you think I will embarrass you, I'm more than happy not to go," I said, hoping for a way out of this evening. The ball had come around far too quickly and while my nights in the forest seemed futile when it came to fulfilling my tasks, I couldn't deny how much I enjoyed being among the trees and plants there. Perhaps simply being alone in nature, even faery-tainted nature, reminded me of home.

"Don't be silly," Marigold protested. "We are going to have so much fun." She turned to Lassila, who was already in the most stunning dress I'd ever seen. It was an A-line ball gown with a corset adorned with the daintiest flowers, in shades of twilight. The skirts that flowed from it were endless layers of tulle, which moved lightly, as Lassila did. Her wings were no longer hidden, stretched out like sheer lace shimmering with diamonds. In her hand she held her mask, which had flowers to match the corset. She looked exquisite.

Marigold was dressed as ever in shades of gold. Her capped sleeves ran down to a shimmering bodice, embroidered with elaborate patterns. Her full skirts were plain, save for the single twirling of thread stitched through, that sparkled like sunshine itself. At her back, net wings gave the illusion that she was as much a faery as her companion, but though they were pretty, they lacked the same magnificence.

"Bring perfume." Lassila nodded at Nyla who disappeared briefly, returning with a bottle that she splashed all over me until my eyes watered.

"It'll have to do," Lassila sighed. "Get her dressed. The carriage will be here momentarily, Marigold, go and wait for it."

Nyla practically charged at me with material that was slipped over my head before I could object. Just like the other dress that Marigold had given me, it fitted perfectly, though we had very different physiques. Some enchantment on the garments must make them fit whoever was wearing them. I didn't mind—it was a ravishing gown, the fabric so light against my skin it was the merest brush of silk. The cream bodice had impossibly fresh wildflowers stitched over it, like a summer meadow, and they trailed onto the tulle skirt. At my back, I could feel the weight of the gauze wings sewn into the bodice, transforming me into a true faery princess. As a little girl, I'd dreamed endlessly about wearing something so beautiful, but now all I could think was how I'd rather be in my old linen dress trampling through nettles in the forest.

Nyla took one look at my hair and gave up, thus I was presented to Lassila, who declared, "It will not do. Fetch me a glamour. I will not be seen with her."

Her comment stung. I loved what I was wearing and thought it was pretty, but clearly I didn't measure up to the exacting standards of Lady Lindelburr.

Nyla tucked a rosebud into my hair, and though I wasn't aware of any change, there obviously was one, because Lassila seemed satisfied.

"Oh, we have matching flowers," Marigold said when we joined her outside, pointing to a white spray in her curls. My heart fell. It was bad enough knowing the true nature of her relationship to Lassila, but witnessing how the faery was using glamours on her only added to the cruelty.

Marigold chatted incessantly on the short carriage ride to the palace. Conor had laughed when I told him I was going to a ball, but he'd also warned me to be careful, reminding me to trust no one. I wondered what he'd think of me dressed like this. Would he see through the glamour, or would I appear unrecognizable to him?

We arrived at a palace entrance I hadn't seen before. A huge swathe of masked faeries were walking through an archway covered in sprawling roses, as our carriage pulled up alongside it.

"Masks on," Lassila instructed.

I looked at mine, plain cream with flowers embroidered on it, and wondered how it would stay in place. There was no ribbon, no tie of any kind. But I watched as Lassila and Marigold pressed them to their faces and copied. The mask stayed in place as though an invisible thread wrapped about my head.

Taking care not to catch our wings on the door, Marigold and I stepped from the carriage and followed Lassila.

Marigold slipped her arm through mine. "I do hope that Ketter Bonberry is here tonight. He danced with me at the last two balls and I think he might have taken a fancy to me."

I glanced at her, noting the flush on her cheeks. "And the feeling is mutual?"

"He's very handsome and looking for a wife, I believe," she replied. "Lassila tells me all the most eligible bachelors want a human wife, we're quite the prize. I'm sure you'll have many interested gentlemen begging you to dance this evening."

"I am far too young to be thinking of marriage and I'm certainly not some object to be obtained," I said, but softened immediately because it was impossible to be cross with Marigold. The way her face fell made me feel as though I'd kicked a kitten. "If dancing the night away with Ketter Bonberry is what you wish, then I hope it comes true."

Beyond the arch was a hallway that would not be out of place in any palace — except it had neither walls nor ceiling. Marble pillars soared pointlessly into the sky, gold framed portraits floated in the air attached to nothing. Floral garlands marked the edge of a path, which was a river of leaves.

We followed the crowd of masked guests to a vast spiral staircase, which led down into the ballroom.

Though this was still open air, there were walls made of hedgerows and filled with every flower imaginable, blooms so small they were barely there, while others stretched wider than my arms, and I breathed in their sweet fragrance. I looked up at the clear sky and smiled at the two full moons and the scarlet stars scattered about them. Beneath the trees, I saw only the glow of their light, and I'd almost forgotten how beautiful they were.

A string quartet played a dulcet tune while upon the dance floor dozens of couples swirled and floated to the dazzling music, each gown spinning past me more entrancing than the last.

And in that moment, in this magical place, I forgot why I would ever want to leave.

# ELEVEN

**M**arigold squeezed my arm, bringing me back to myself. "There he is!" she squealed, nodding at a faery with hair as golden as hers. His low-cut emerald shirt shimmered like tansy beetles, and his pants were the color of twilight. What I could see of his face beneath the mask suggested he was every bit as handsome as all the other fae.

"Isn't he wonderful?" Marigold breathed as he noticed her and waved, a wily smile creeping to his lips.

"He certainly seems happy to see you," I said, and I was glad for her.

"Good evening, Miss Marigold," Ketter said, bowing low. "And who is your companion?"

"This is my friend, Nettle," Marigold said, and I politely said hello.

"I do not wish to interrupt, but I was wondering if I might have this dance?" Ketter asked Marigold.

"Would you mind terribly if I abandoned you?" she asked me.

"Not at all," I assured her.

Marigold took Ketter's hand, and they disappeared onto the dance floor. There was no sign of Lassila, who, of course, had no intention of spending the evening with me. I wondered what to do.

I hadn't wanted to come, had agreed because Marigold had been kind to me and I didn't want to be rude. Standing alone now, surrounded by the beauty of this place, the gloriousness of the music and the exquisiteness of the gowns, I felt suddenly exposed. I didn't belong here. I couldn't let the magic seduce me, trick me into forgetting who I was and what mattered to me.

I skirted the edge of the ballroom, moving against the crowd, trying to make my way to the spiral staircase. But as I reached it a strange sensation washed over me, giving me pause.

I didn't want to leave, that was a foolish notion. I should stay and dance.

With a sigh of happiness, I began to waltz, though I had no partner, nor any previous knowledge of the steps, but I skipped my way into a quieter corner and danced alone in the shadows. I shut my eyes and lost myself to the bewitching melody, giddy with delight, and ready to spin until my feet bled.

A cool hand, soft as velvet, slipped into mine, as a strong arm slid around my waist, forcing me to slow down. I opened my eyes and was surprised to find myself pressed close to Ellion. Even with a mask, it was so obviously him, with his permanent scowl and perfect jawline.

"What are you doing here, Nettle?" he spoke low into my ear.

"How did you know it was me?" I teased. "I am disguised so well."

"I would recognize you anywhere."

It was oddly satisfying to know the glamour hadn't worked on him.

"I thought you'd be out in the woods, but I suppose I should have known you'd give up on your task so quickly."

"I haven't given up," I said. "I'm taking a night off. And you're the ones cheating."

"Yes, how are you getting along with your knife?" he asked slyly.

"I'll have you know I've already worked my way round that," I replied, wishing he'd be quiet so I could focus on the music. "I've been cutting the stems, I just can't collect them in your stupid enchanted sack. But you already know that."

"You've cut them?" His whole manner changed. "How?"

I laughed, my head light and dizzy. "Wouldn't you like to know?"

He stopped dancing and held me firmly. "Yes, I would."

I managed to extract my hand to tap him on the nose. "You have your secrets," I said. "And I have mine."

Ellion sighed. "You must have been enchanted. I think it's time for you to go. Come, you'll thank me tomorrow."

He took my elbow and led me toward the far corner of the room. It was only then I noticed how nicely he was dressed, his long black coat sparkling with silver dust, his black pants embroidered with silver thread. I looked up at him and smiled. "You really like black, don't you? You have a whole brooding thing going on."

Ellion ignored me, and I realized I didn't care. I wanted to dance more, so I tugged his arm, trying to urge him to return to the floor with me.

But he was far stronger and when we reached the corner, he pulled me through a gap in the walls, where the music faded and darkness gathered about us.

"Time to wake up," he commanded.

"I am awake," I said. "And I want to dance."

"You are being ridiculous," he growled, not grasping that the more frustrated he grew, the more I was entertained.

I darted out of his grip and started to run into the shadows. "If you want to make me leave, you'll have to catch me!" I closed my eyes as I abandoned myself to the caress of the cool night air.

"Nettle!" Ellion's angry voice rang out, but when he called again, it sounded distant and I opened my eyes.

I was no longer in the same place, but in a room formed from granite standing stones. In between were trees that looked in almost every way like silver birch, but with long weeping branches like a willow, the silver leaves crystallized as though caught in a frost. At the far end from where I stood, was a vast mirror in a frame that seemed to be made of twisted bones, supported by two antlers and adorned with primroses. In the middle of the room was a throne of crumbling stone, moss and lichen spreading from every nook and cranny.

But it was the man kneeling at the foot of the mirror who drew my attention.

Locryn was staring at the reflection of the most beautiful woman I had ever seen. Her gown was made of spun web, her tumbled hair a million silver leaves, her skin flawless, a smile more precious than jewels on her lips. Upon her head was a crown of bone and ice and her power radiated even from this distance.

The king reached to press his hand to the glass.

"Keita," he cried, and the pain in his voice startled me. "Come back to me, my love."

His queen appeared not to be able to hear him, for she began to speak and laugh, though no sound was audible, and I understood this was a mirror like the ones in the shop I'd seen. Was this a memory from his past, or a dream relived?

"Why do you torture me?" Locryn asked the figure, who was now dancing with several other faeries in a scene of perfect bliss. His lament turned to rage and he smashed his fist against the glass. "Don't torment me, this cannot be real. You cannot be happy while I suffer." He pounded again at the glass. "Keita!"

I would have intruded upon this private moment longer, but someone grabbed me and pulled me back into the shadows.

The next thing I knew, I was back in my stable with a furious Ellion.

"Are you trying to get us both killed?"

He reached to remove the rosebud from my hair, and immediately whatever enchantment had settled on me lifted. But remembering how I had danced with Ellion, I blushed. I had enjoyed it, enchanted or not.

"A cheap spell," he said, crushing it under his foot. "To control as well as glamour you."

I should have known.

Ellion wasn't concerned about Lassila's trickery though. "How did you get into the king's private chamber?"

"I don't know," I said. "One minute I was running from you, next I was there. Perhaps another path altering my direction."

Ellion's head tilted. "Like in the forest?"

I shrugged.

"You'd better be careful," he said. "If the king had found you there before I did, no excuse would have saved you."

"I don't understand," I said, removing my mask. "Why wasn't he at the ball?"

Ellion started to pace, as if wondering how much to share with me. He really did look devastatingly dashing in his fancy clothes. After a deep sigh, he turned to me. "When the king and queen parted, Keita banished Locryn from her lands entirely. Locryn never told anyone why, but whatever he did to anger her must have been terrible, because she set an enchantment against his magic, forbidding him ever to return. All he has left is that mirror, a cruel parting gift from her. It allows him a constant window into her life where she is always happy. It drives him to madness, knowing that she thrives without him, while no matter how many balls he throws, he cannot find a moment's relief from his misery."

"He wants her back."

Ellion nodded. "They have always fought, have frequently had spells apart after some argument or other, but they have always reconciled. I'm not sure what hurts him most, that she has spurned him so violently, or that he still cares. I often wonder if he saw her again, would he wish to win her back, or pay her back."

I recalled how Locryn had veered from sorrow to fury and wasn't sure either.

"You must be close for him to confide in you," I said. The last thing I was expecting was for Ellion to laugh.

"Close? No, he despises me. I'm a changeling who returned, tainted by the touch of the human world. That's why I'm assigned demeaning tasks."

I raised my eyebrow. "Like looking after me?"

He nodded. "Exactly. I told you, I'm a loner."

The silver in his dark eyes shimmered, drawing me to them. The king might not value Ellion, but I liked him. He was difficult and sullen, but there was something in those eyes that beckoned me in a way that had nothing to do with magic—

"Wait," I said, a thought occurring suddenly. "If you're not his friend, then how do you know all this about him? How do you know how he feels about his queen?"

Ellion smiled then, full of mischief, as he stepped backwards into the gloom.

"Because Locryn forgets one very important thing," he said. "I can see everything from the shadows." And with that he disappeared into what remained of the night.

# TWELVE

That was how time passed. During the sunlight, I worked with Conor, and occasionally visited Marigold and Lassila. Through the long hours of moonlight, I pointlessly hacked at nettles, unless I was attending the masquerade balls, where Ellion would always end up grudgingly dancing with me to keep me from trouble.

It was hard to have any measure of how long it had been since I'd fallen into the realm and whenever I tried, my thoughts grew misty. All I could hope was that Locryn had suspended time to keep Grandma safe, and if he had chosen not to, that it hadn't been as long for her, that she and the animals still lived.

Conor had grown used to my presence and made me laugh. I enjoyed being with him and the horses. Pym had quickly become my favorite with her moody attitude. She still pretended to bite me, but never caught my skin. I think she liked me but wanted to protect her feisty reputation.

Marigold was always welcoming whenever I visited, though Lassila and I continued in our mutual dislike. Lassila was far from happy about Marigold's blossoming relationship with Ketter, and I worried that Marigold's memories of him might start to fade. The Bonberrys were a powerful faery family though, and I hoped Lassila's mischief might be tempered by not wishing to make an enemy of them.

The masquerades were something I both anticipated and dreaded in equal measure. I loved wearing gorgeous gowns and was always swept away by the breathtaking beauty of the whole affair, but every night spent there was a night not spent cutting nettles.

Completing my task seemed depressingly out of reach. The forest continued to take me on random paths in defiance of Gammi's magical thread, but it did at least bring me to dense nettle patches, and at dawn, always released me.

I listened constantly for the voice, which had called to me previously and led me to the leaflings, but it never came. Its absence left me lonely among the trees.

On an unusually stormy night, I shivered in my soaked dress, cutting nettles as the rain poured down. My fingers were so cold I could barely hold the penknife, and I had to force myself to keep going through sheer stubbornness.

*What's the point?* I wondered, as I cut my finger on the sharp leaves, so numb I'd grown clumsy. I kicked the hessian sack, which mocked me with its emptiness. *Time after time, for what? You're never going to fill up.*

I slumped to the wet forest floor, too tired even for tears. I was beyond exhausted—how long could I keep doing this? Crawling forward, I curled up among the nettles, drinking in their familiar scent, not caring that they scratched me. This was where I had always gone for comfort, and I needed it now more than ever.

Almost immediately, my mood calmed. The air seemed easier to breathe, the urgency to save my grandma diminished. Panic melted away and surrounded by nettles, I returned to myself, my head clearer than ever.

I just had to think. I'd found a way to cut the nettles in the first place. It stood to reason there must be a way to overcome the sack's enchantment. Perhaps Gammi had something on her stall that could help? Or another of the stall-holders. I still had some candy I could trade, though I imagined they were getting sticky by now.

My hand felt for them in my pocket, and yes, my fingers touched some oozing wrappers. Not that I thought Gammi would mind. Then my fingers brushed against something else, and I sat bolt upright.

There was the horseshoe that I had slipped in on that fateful evening. A horseshoe made of iron. Surely if anything could break a faery enchantment, it was that?

Scrambling out of the nettles, I snatched up the sack and threw the horseshoe into it. Nothing happened. I shook the sack, feeling the weight of the iron crescent in the bottom. It hadn't disappeared. Feverishly, I started cutting more stems and bundled them in.

They lay at the bottom of the bag, as visible as when they had been in my hand.

"Ahhh!" I cried out, throwing my head back in the rain. "I did it!" I began to cut more stems, desperate to fill the sack in case there was some time limit to the iron's power.

It didn't take long until nettle stalks were poking out of the top — no one could argue the sack wasn't full to bursting. After popping in a few more for extra measure, I dragged the sack behind me, practically running through the woodland toward the palace.

Mercifully, the rain had ceased by the time I made it back, the clouds separating to reveal the moons in their radiance, but I was soaking wet. It occurred to me, as I traipsed about looking for an entrance, that I had no idea how to find the throne room again to present the nettles. Ellion had been quite specific that to complete the task that was what I had to do.

Searching for some shadows, I headed toward them. I would need help for this next part.

"Can you hear me?" I spoke into the darkness.

"Unfortunately." Ellion stepped from the shadows as if he had always been there. He looked me up and down, and wasn't impressed by the soggy mess before him. "What do you want?"

"You told me to bring the full sack of nettles before the throne," I said, trying to stop my teeth from chattering. "So here I am."

With bored disinterest, Ellion glanced at what I was holding. Then his eyes widened.

"You did it?" He couldn't believe it.

"Told you I'd find a way," I beamed, feeling smug.

The corner of Ellion's mouth tugged upwards. Was that a smile? It faded as quickly as it had appeared. "You'd better come with me."

At the wave of his hand, an opening appeared among the overgrown ivy on the wall of the palace, and I hurried after him, noting that as soon as we were inside, the gap closed behind us. Leaving wet footprints in my wake, I followed Ellion through corridors that reminded me of ancient ruins on the moors, crumbling stone swallowed by brambles and briars—and yet here didn't seem a forgotten echo of the past but a glorious architectural decision.

A small door opened as Ellion approached, leading us into the throne room, where a very angry-looking king was perched on his throne.

"You'd better have good reason to have brought her here," Locryn shouted at Ellion. "Cover her at once."

This time I was prepared for the spiders that lowered and spun their veil over my face. When they withdrew, Locryn gestured for me to approach. He was dressed in all his finery, his crown beaded with dewdrops, his pants dazzling like starlight, and I wondered how someone so beautiful on the outside could be so cruel within.

"I've brought you this, Your Majesty," I said, placing the sack in front of me.

Locryn stared from it, to me, and I feared he might explode with rage. Instead, he laughed, but there was no humor there.

"What would possess you to come here with such a pathetic gift?" asked Locryn, his voice dangerously on edge.

"It is a sack full of nettles," Ellion said. If Locryn was hot anger, Ellion was cold calmness.

"A what?"

"Nettles," I said, lifting the sack. "Just as you asked."

"She has completed her first task, my lord," Ellion said, and at last Locryn understood.

He didn't, however, appear to believe it.

The king stood and stepped toward me. "You? Completed my task?"

I nodded, glad that the veil hid the hair plastered to my face and my nose red with cold. It was hard to stand in the presence of such beauty at the best of times, let alone when I was so bedraggled.

The king looked at Ellion again, who gave a nod of confirmation.

It was hard to read Locryn's expression, but I was certain there was a flash of hope in his eyes before they narrowed in calculation. He stared at me as if I was a riddle to solve, and the air crackled with imminent danger while we awaited his judgement.

Finally, Locryn seemed to make a decision, because he returned to his throne. "Do you know how many humans have ever succeeded in completing my tasks?"

"Seeing as you cheat to make them impossible, I'm guessing none?" I regretted my careless tongue almost immediately.

"You dare to call me a cheat? You think the King of the Moorland a liar?"

He was trying to intimidate me and though it was working, I held my ground. "I think you are clever with your words and like to win. But I am sure you would always honor a deal, even if it was with a human."

"Yes," the king said, before smiling. "And no. There is always time for one last renegotiation."

My blood chilled.

"But let's not talk about that yet," he continued. "As I recall, you agreed to complete three tasks for me, not one. The next will not be easy."

The first had hardly been a stroll in the park. I tipped my chin defiantly. "I'm ready."

Locryn smiled. "Are you?" He was mocking me, I was certain of it. "We shall see."

With that, we were dismissed. I picked up the nettles, assuming Locryn didn't want to keep them.

Ellion didn't speak as he escorted me through the

palace. I wasn't sure whether I'd done something to upset him, but there was a pronounced tension in the air. Perhaps he was cross with me for talking back to the king and was preparing to chide me for my stupidity.

"Do you know what my next task is?" I asked him, as I struggled to keep up with his long stride.

He ignored me.

"Ugh, you faeries and your secrets. It's not very nice to hide things from me, you know."

He remained silent, so I gave up, until I realized we weren't returning to the stable or the yard, but were heading instead toward a stone barn.

"Where are we?" I asked, looking about for anything familiar and discovering I'd entirely lost my bearings.

"Your new home." Ellion paused at the door. "This is where you are to work on your next task."

I frowned in confusion. "Which is?"

"You are to fashion a garment for the king."

I stared at Ellion before I laughed. When he didn't join in, I quickly stopped. "Oh, you're not joking. I can't make him anything. Well, not anything he'd want to wear. I made this." I gestured to my soaked dress. "Why would he want me to make anything?"

Ellion looked like a man whose patience was wearing thin. "You wished to know your next task. I have told you."

"Right." I tried to think. I did at least know how to do this. Although at home I had my sewing machine, even if it was as old as my grandma. "I have to make him a garment. Anything more specific? Does he want pants? A whole outfit? I know he won't want a shirt."

Ellion gave me a withering glance. "Make what you want. The only condition is that you create it from these."

He pushed the barn door open.

My jaw dropped at the sight before me. The room was filled from top to bottom with nettle stems, smelling as fresh as the day they were picked, and a horrible realization dawned on me.

"They're the ones I cut, aren't they?" I asked. "They weren't disappearing into thin air, the sack was transporting them here."

Ellion nodded.

"You want me to turn these into clothing?"

He nodded again.

"How?" The word caught in my throat as panic gripped me.

Ellion rested his hands on my shoulders, forcing me to face him. "You should not have been able to cut the nettles, but you did. You should not have been able to fill the sack, but you did. I know Locryn. This is not a random assignment."

His eyes glimmered in the last of the moonlight and I tried hard to focus on his words, but all I could think about was the gentle touch of his hands through my wet dress.

"I have no idea how to do what he's asked," I said, trembling from cold and fear.

"Not yet. You don't strike me as someone who gives up though," Ellion said. "Be careful, Nettle. Don't trust the king."

"I don't trust any faery," I whispered.

"Not even me?"

Our faces were close, and his lips mesmerized me. I imagined how they would feel pressed against mine. "Especially not you."

He smiled, just the smallest hint, but undeniable. I lifted my gaze from his lips to his eyes and lost myself in their shine.

Suddenly I became aware that I was no longer cold, my clothes and hair no longer wet. He'd used magic. Had that moment between us been real or a trick? "You enchanted me?"

"Only a drying spell," he said. "I promise I have changed nothing about you." He hesitated, before adding, "Why would I want to?"

And he left me, speechless, breathless, utterly alone.

# THIRTEEN

I fell asleep among the nettles. Bone-weary, I hollowed out a space to curl into, and abandoned myself to oblivion.

I dreamed of silver bells ringing, I heard my name carried on the wind—and I followed it. I floated through a white forest, the papery trunks of thousands of silver birch illuminated in a wash of crimson moonlight. The voice led me to a glade cloaked in mist. Through the haze I saw a figure. She wasn't facing me, but was wearing a simple green gown, her tousled raven locks spilling down her back.

"Hello?" I called. She didn't react to my presence, perhaps unaware of me. "Are you all right?" I asked, moving closer. "Can I help you?"

The woman's arms wrapped protectively around herself as she sobbed and an overwhelming urge to comfort her came over me.

# Nettle

"It's okay," I said, understanding the ache that came from struggling alone. It was, after all, what had driven me to this place. "I'm here."

She turned and the tear-stained face before me was mine. Or a strange kind of reflection of my own. Looking right through me, as if I were the dream and not her, she whispered to the night.

"Help me."

I wanted to reassure her, promise I would if only she'd tell me how, but the mist thickened until I lost sight of her and all I could hear were the bells once more and that voice.

*Nettle.*

---

When I awoke, my heart was pounding, my skin damp with sweat. I hadn't dreamed since arriving here, but now the image of the woman — of me — crying refused to fade.

Sitting up, I stared at the thousands of nettle stems surrounding me and sighed. Was the scale of the challenge before me leaving me so desperate, I was searching for answers in my sleep?

I doubted any advice would have included me sitting around all day worrying. I ran my fingers through my tangled hair and headed out, ready to find my way to the yard. There were stables to clean, horses to groom, Conor to help.

The barn was in a meadow by itself, so I followed the path Ellion had brought me along, reasoning that it would take me back to the palace, and I could find my way from there. I was bewildered to find myself in a walled garden instead, where raised beds overflowed with vegetables, and fruits of every kind grew on trees and up canes.

"Why do you keep messing with me?" I grumbled out loud to the pathways, holding up my wrist. "This is supposed to stop you from doing that."

As I walked through the garden, admiring the unfamiliar berries in shades of blue and green, I started smiling. There truly was so much beauty here and every new corner seemed to hold some unexpected discovery.

*You could just stay here. You would be happy.*

I shook the thought away. That was the allure of the faery magic permeating the air, intending to trap me, keep me prisoner. I wanted to go home, I wanted to save Grandma, and I forced those goals into the forefront of my mind. I mustn't lose myself to this place.

Eventually, I found my way to the yard, where Conor was busy at work.

He gave me a crooked smile as I approached, and something lifted inside me. After a lifetime of people turning away at my arrival, or poorly hiding their whispers of derision, his smile was welcome.

"You finally managed to get some sleep?" he asked, with a grin. So he'd noticed how I was awake most of the time then? Maybe he'd found it hard to rest when he first arrived here too, where nothing was quite usual.

"A little," I said, not wanting to mention the strange dream. With Conor I preferred not to dwell on the magic of this place. Though his memory of our world was very different to mine, he did recall some of it, and more than that, he wanted to. Going home had been his dream for many lifetimes.

"I filled the sack," I said to him, trying not to sound too triumphant. I knew the impossibility of his own task weighed heavily on him.

Conor frowned, not really listening. "What sack?"

"For the nettles. I filled it and presented it to the king." Now I couldn't help the smile that spread across my face. "I completed my first task."

That got his attention. His eyes darted to mine. "You did it?" When I nodded, he could scarcely believe it. "How?"

So I explained what I'd done, how I'd used iron again to block the magic they were using, how the king had been his usual tricksy self, and how I was now supposed to fashion a garment out of nettles as my next task.

"I don't think iron is going to help me this time," I sighed. "I don't have any idea how to do what he's asked."

"Could you knit them?" Conor suggested, and at the thought of Locryn wearing a leafy knitted scarf, I burst out laughing. "Perhaps not," Conor agreed, shaking his head. "Sorry, I know as much about turning plants into clothing as you do."

"It's okay," I said. "I'll figure something out. I did before."

This time, Conor's smile was sad. "Aye, you did."

I stepped closer to him, understanding his sorrow. "The tasks aren't impossible, Conor. You mustn't give up hope."

"Hope is dangerous, Nettle. Do you know how many times I've attempted my task? More nights than you've drawn breath. Every time, it defeats me. Not the task itself, but that moment, that brief incredible moment where I think that maybe, just maybe, this time I'm going to do it. And then, when I don't? Well, every failure cuts deeper than the last." He sighed. "I guard my hope now. It isn't boundless and without it, I won't survive here."

I didn't know what to say. I wanted to take his hand to comfort him, but it seemed too intimate a gesture, and I feared he might interpret it as pity. More than that, I feared he might push me away.

So I said nothing. He was right, I didn't know what it must be like to live here so long and watch each chance to leave repeatedly slip away.

I could see him trying to shrug off his despair, though his smile was untypically strained. "Want to help me shovel manure?"

"That's an offer a girl can't refuse." I was happy for the mood to be lightened and found solace in the familiar work of mucking out.

Even so, I couldn't stop thinking about the barn full of nettles and as I worked, I came up with a plan for how to proceed with the task given to me. Well, more a starting point, but it was all I had—when the sun set and the moons rose, I slipped out of the palace grounds and headed toward the night market.

The sweet scent of spices filled my nose as soon as I approached, the music enfolding me in its embrace. I didn't bother to fight it and skipped through the crowds, resisting the temptations on display. There was only one stall I was interested in.

Gammi's eyes widened with hungry glee when she caught sight of me, and she lunged forwards. "I wondered when I'd be seeing you again. What do you need? You tell Gammi, she'll sort you out."

"You sold me some faulty thread," I said, hoping I sounded firm, but not rude.

"Tsk. Nonsense," she responded dismissively.

"It was supposed to stop the paths shifting on me in the forest and yet they keep doing it. It happens at the palace too. It's faulty and I want a replacement."

Gammi grabbed my wrist and studied the thread closely, her brow knotting. "Nonsense," she repeated. "The charm still holds."

"I'm not lying, I promise you. It doesn't work."

Gammi looked up at me, tilting her head. "Or is it you that is the problem?"

"Me?" That took me by surprise. "I have simply been going about my business, it's your product that has let me down. But I would be willing to overlook it in exchange for some information."

Her eyes narrowed, and I could tell she was as tempted to make a deal as everyone else here. "What are you wanting to know?"

"Do you make the threads you sell?"

Her face scrunched up in surprise. "What kind of a question is that? Course I do."

"How?" When she looked at me blankly, I added, 'What do you make them from? Plants? Leaves?"

Now she looked confused. "Magic," she said as if it was the most obvious thing in the world. "Here, try this." She thrust a knotted handful of golden thread toward me. "Tie that round your ankles and you'll dance all night without growing tired." She wiggled her eyebrows persuasively.

"I need to know how to turn plants into cloth," I said. "Can you help me?"

Gammi looked disappointed. "No," she said eventually, sounding dejected. But then an idea occurred to her, and she perked up. "I could point you in the right direction though."

"You could?" My own hopes raised.

"For the right price." Gammi stared at me, and I knew what she demanded.

I pulled out a sticky sherbet, holding it out of her reach. "Tell me what you know, and it's yours."

"Seems to me the place to start is to talk to someone who makes clothes," Gammi said, not taking her eyes from the candy. "There are those here who barter cloth, but they won't be able to help you. No, you want to go to someone with true knowledge."

"Who?"

"In the forest, find the emerald river." She tied dark green thread, which briefly seared my skin, around my thumb. "This will lead you. Where the river forks, you'll find the entrance to her workshop. You'll know it when you see it." She tried to grab the sherbet, but I held it higher.

"Whose workshop?"

"The royal seamstress of course," Gammi replied. "Now give me that."

I let her take it and didn't wait for her to demand a second. I hurried back through the marketplace purposefully. I'd thought my long nights in the forest were over after finally cutting the nettles.

But it looked as though fate had other ideas.

※

The crimson moon was low in the sky, bigger and brighter than its silver sister. Even in the shelter of the forest, I could sense its strength and welcomed its light.

Given how ineffective the other thread was, I didn't have high hopes. So it was a pleasant surprise to discover that I seemed to know exactly which way to go at every bend and twist in the path, and even when it shifted, I felt I was going in the right direction. As I walked, I passed through a glade carpeted with tiny silver flowers, their dainty heads like bells. In the moonlight, they glowed bright, and as a rush of wind passed over them, they rang with the tuneless song I'd heard so many times in my dreams.

Fascinated, I brushed my palm across the top of the petals, intrigued to find them cold to the touch. My fingers traced a stem, and I was seized by an impulse to pick it.

Upon doing so, a thunderous storm broke fast and furious in my head. The ringing of bells was unbearable—a deafening cacophony. I clutched my temples, desperate for relief from the noise.

Gradually, the roar faded into the wind as I lay on the ground, gasping for breath. Slowly, I sat up, staring at the flower, which was already wilting in my hand. How could so small and dainty a thing have caused so much torment?

I should have known. Nothing here could be trusted.

Staggering back to my feet, I carried on my way. I'd been foolish to deviate from the task at hand and could imagine what Conor would say if he learned of my stupidity. Not that he would.

I heard the river before I saw it—the gentle burble of water running over rock—and hurried on. True to its name, it was a dazzling emerald green, carving through the forest. Leaflings skated on its surface and fluttered away at my appearance.

A strange urge to paddle came over me and I was about to dip my toes when I caught hold of myself. Had I not just learned that any unusual desire here meant some harm would befall me should I surrender to it? So I resisted, no matter how refreshing the water looked, and followed it along, searching for the fork.

I didn't have to walk far. As the forest dipped downhill, the river spilled in a waterfall over a granite wall, which divided its flow into two streams. It was there I could see the entrance, as Gammi had said it would be.

It wasn't easy to reach, I had to shuffle carefully along a damp edge, trying to avoid being splashed. Up closer, I could see a gap between the stones, leading into gloomy darkness.

That was where I had to go.

Grateful once again for the way my eyes adjusted so readily to the change in light, I waited a bit, and there it was. A narrow stairway winding down.

It was possible that some day I might not wander blindly into dangerous situations. But as the sound of the water hitting rock rushed past me, I knew one thing with absolute certainty.

It wouldn't be today.

# FOURTEEN

The steps were slippery, the air growing colder, but there was a distant light in this underground lair, and I followed it like a moth drawn to a flame.

Since Gammi had first mentioned the royal seamstress, I'd wondered what I might find. Another faery? A hobgoblin like Gammi herself? Maybe it would be an exceptionally skilled human who had carved their place here. It hadn't occurred to me to consider whether they might pose any threat to me. I suppose I'd imagined anyone who possessed the creativity and skill to make beautiful garments couldn't possibly be bad.

Now, in this damp and unpleasant place, I wasn't so sure.

As I approached the light, I became aware of a humming noise, a constant drone, and I brushed past curtains of cobwebs toward it.

Nothing could have prepared me for what lay behind them.

The cavern was vast and thick with shining web draped in every direction, the lantern light reflecting off the fine strands and illuminating the space, where hundreds of oversized flies busily worked. Watching them were hordes of large spiders, and everywhere the most resplendent gowns I'd ever seen, in every stage of production.

I was in awe of the sheer scale of it, struck by the artistry of the garments. But as my eyes attuned to the dancing light, I paid more attention to what the flies were doing as they carefully picked their way along the sticky web.

Some were plucking the spots from ladybugs' backs, others were pulling the iridescent wings off beetles. Birds in cages were singing silent tunes, and many had bald patches where their feathers had been removed. Hardly audible beneath the hum of the flies' wings, I could hear tiny screams echo through the cave, and the stale stench of death was unmistakable.

I should not have come here.

"No!" The angry voice reverberated around the cave, drowning all other sound. I looked to see who had shouted.

Instantly, I wished I hadn't. A spider bigger than the others was giving orders. She wore a wispy lace shawl that spooled onto the ground, and she was gesturing at a sketch on the table before her.

"That is ordinary, it will not do. It must be radiant, exceptional. Starlings' tears. Or the promise of dawn. Must I think of everything?"

The spider she spoke to cowered and rolled up the sketch, hurrying away. Then the spider in charge, who I could only assume was the royal seamstress, began an inspection of the gowns in progress.

She approached some flies who were stitching moss to a bodice. "That isn't neat enough." She fixed eight glistening beady eyes on them. "Do it again."

Moving on, she paused at a skirt, where the flies were applying some kind of dye to turn it red. They buzzed nervously as the spider examined their work.

"More blood," she commanded. "Now!"

To my horror, a piercing scream filled the air and moments later another fly brought over a bowl filled with fresh blood. I was glad I hadn't seen the creature it had come from. I could only hope it survived.

The spider moved past a few more worktables before she reached a fly who was pinning live butterflies to a neckline, their fragile wings flapping in desperation. When the spider came to a halt, I thought perhaps she was going to do something to save them. Instead, she glared at the fly. "You have smudged the dust on this butterfly's wing. The gown is ruined."

"I'm sorry," the fly buzzed. "I will put it right."

"You have had more than one warning," the spider replied. "This is the last time you will fail me." Swiftly, she tugged on a strand of web, pulling the fly straight into her open fangs, swallowing him whole.

That was enough for me. I would find another way to learn how to complete my task. This was far too dangerous, and I couldn't quite believe Gammi had sent me here.

I turned to leave, hoping to sneak away unnoticed, but my foot caught on some web and sent a shockwave through the whole cavern, the web bouncing to alert my presence. Everyone froze, and I wasn't sure who was more shocked, them or me. Before I could do anything, the giant spider had me in her sights.

Moving with exceptional speed, her long legs reached for me. "What possesses you to enter my lair?"

Somehow holding my nerve, I faced her as bravely as I could. "I'm here on palace business," I said. "I wish to speak to the royal seamstress."

"I am Beattie," she replied. "And I have no interest in what a shadow faery wants."

"Ellion didn't send me," I assured her. "I am here on behalf of the king. He has tasked me with making him a garment and—"

She raised a large hairy leg in front of my face to silence me. "Did my ears deceive me? It sounded as though you said the king asked you—*you*—to make him clothes?"

I nodded. "He did."

"No one makes clothes for the king apart from me," she said, every word a warning. "Who else knows how to embellish cuffs with the glow of a thousand fireflies, or thread a nightingale's song through a skirt?" She cast me a look of repulsion. "Not you, I'd wager."

So much bloodshed, so much suffering, and for what? An eye-catching dress. A dazzling waistcoat. Beauty at a cruel cost. "You're right, I have no idea what I'm doing," I said. "Which is why I need your help."

Beattie eyed me with undisguised contempt. "The king demands magnificence and that is something only I can provide. There is no help I can offer you. Now leave while you still breathe."

I stood my ground. "I didn't ask for this," I insisted. "I'm not trying to replace you, or anything like that. I only need to know how to make something out of nettles."

"Nettles?"

"Yes."

She shook her head as she glowered down at me. "No. They are forbidden plants. Faeries cannot touch them, nor I, nor any creature in this moorland realm. What you suggest is impossible."

"Well, I can assure you I have a whole barn full of stalks that I've cut," I said boldly. "I was wondering whether I could stitch them together. Would that even work, or would it be too fragile?"

Beattie wasn't listening to me though, she was lost in her thoughts. "Could it be done?" she muttered to herself. "Has he found a way?"

I frowned. "A way to do what?"

"This request," she said. "It came from the king himself?"

"Yes, well, through Ellion. My first task was to cut the nettles, my second to fashion a garment from them."

"He must think you can do it," Beattie muttered. "Why, though?" Her probing eyes met my blank ones. "How did you cut the nettles? No one can cut them."

Every instinct warned me not to trust Beattie — my penknife, like my sherbets, might hold some value here. Although as it was made of steel, the iron in it might make it impossible for her to touch. Nevertheless, it wasn't a risk I wished to take.

"Nettle by name, nettle by nature," I said, hoping it sounded cryptic and not nonsensical.

Beattie regarded me even more closely. "You know nothing of your name or nature," she said after a while. "You're as trapped as these flies, caught in a web you can't even see. Tell me, are you sure you wish to do what the king has asked?"

Her insult vexed me. "I made a deal, and this is one of the tasks I must complete."

Her sinister laughter echoed through the cavern. "Poor fool. You are playing a game you cannot win."

"Then there is no harm in telling me what I need to know."

A cunning expression spread across her face. "All right then," she said. "You must turn the nettles into cloth."

My heart began to beat too fast. "I can't do that."

"You cut the nettles, so I think perhaps you can. The question is whether you should."

I was tired of these riddles. "If you have something you want to say, then do." It probably wasn't wise to get cross with a massive spider, but she was either going to help me, or not. And either going to let me live, or not.

Beattie loomed above me, and I thought for certain I had sealed my own fate. But then she said, "What you must do will not be easy. It's not been done before, not to my knowledge. You must strip the leaves from the stalks and extract the fiber from within the stems. Spin it, then weave it. And from the cloth make a garment fit for a king."

I waited for her to elaborate on those instructions, fighting back my rising panic, but she offered no further advice.

"OK, but *how*? I was with you until extracting the fiber... what fiber? Extract it how?" My voice shook with growing hysteria. I'd hoped for answers, not more complications.

"Locryn did not task *me* with this request. *You* cut the nettles, and so *you* must find the solution. Because what you need to understand is this. The clothes I make? They are exquisite, beyond all beauty. Worthy of a royal court. The king demands new items constantly, so that every ball, no one is wearing the same thing again. He desires every dance be more magnificent than the last and I play my part."

Pride glimmered in her many eyes before they narrowed, as her thoughts returned to me.

"That is not what the king wants from you. He does not ask for beauty, or brilliance. You must ask yourself, what *is* it he wants from you? Then you must decide whether you are willing to give it to him. I advise you to think very carefully about your answer." She gestured for me to leave. But as I turned to go, she called out.

"No trespasser has ever left my lair alive. You would be wise to consider why you are an exception."

# FIFTEEN

The rose-gold sun was rising as I returned to the yard, fighting exhaustion.

Conor was climbing down the ladder from his hayloft, his black hair sticking up at all angles.

"Morning," I called to him.

"Hi," he replied, but when he hopped off the ladder and looked properly in my direction, his forehead creased. "You've not slept, have you? Where've you been?"

"Paid a visit to the royal seamstress," I said, hoping he wouldn't ask how such an idea had come to me. "She's told me that I need to turn the nettles to cloth, although she was ridiculously vague about the details."

His eyes widened and he took a breath. "Come on. You need to eat something."

I had no choice but to do as I was told as he ushered me back into his hayloft and gave me a plate of shredded red leaves. While I ate, he said nothing, but once I'd finished, he could keep quiet no longer.

"You're not taking care of yourself," he said, and his concern both touched and irritated me.

"I'm all right."

"You're barely sleeping, you barely eat. I know being here makes those things seem less important, but do you know who doesn't need to sleep? Who doesn't have to eat? Faeries! It's absurd how they mimic humans because it's fashionable, yet they despise us, consider us lesser beings."

His anger silenced me. It had seemed so natural to keep pushing myself that I hadn't questioned what that might mean.

"You're right," I said. "I'll try harder to force myself to remember I'm human."

Conor fixed his most furious stare on me. "Good, because you are making poor choices."

My temper flared and I folded my arms. "Such as?"

"What were you thinking? Going to Beattie's lair. Do you know how dangerous that is? How are you not dead?"

"I didn't realize how bad an idea it was until I was there," I said, knowing it was a feeble explanation. "Look, the main thing is, I am still alive."

"What possessed you to go there? How did you even know about it?"

So I told him everything, how Gammi had sent me there, what Beattie had told me, and by the end of it, Conor was more angry than ever.

"Look, I like Gammi. But you can't trust her. She doesn't care whether you survive or not. What do I keep telling you, Nettle? Don't trust anyone here!"

He was pacing now and it amused me.

"I trust you," I said.

That stopped him in his tracks and he looked at me, those blue eyes shining like a summer sky.

"Then, please," he said. "Be more careful. I haven't had a friend in a long time, I don't want to lose you."

I stood up and stepped toward him. "You won't, Conor," I promised.

His eyes searched mine, and then to my astonishment, he pulled me into a clumsy hug. "I mean it," he whispered. "You *have* to be careful."

He released me enough so that our faces were close, our eyes fixed on each other's. There was such tenderness in his expression, such kindness, and I leaned toward him, dropping my gaze to his lips as they moved to meet mine.

The clatter of hooves shattered the moment.

"Conor! Where are you?" Morcan's voice brought us back to earth, and we moved apart, both laughing shyly.

"No rest for the wicked," he said. "Let's go and sort out the horses." I hung back, and when he turned to look, I saw understanding pass across his face. "You're not coming, are you?"

"I'm sorry," I said, shaking my head. "Beattie gave me a place to start; I have to do what I can."

Conor gave a short nod. "Of course. I understand. But we'll miss you."

"You'll be glad to have some peace and quiet," I said, but though he laughed, the last thing I saw before he disappeared down the ladder was his face knotted with disappointment.

I tried not to think about our almost-kiss as I made my way back to the barn. I tried not to think about Beattie devouring the fly who'd failed her, about the creatures she tortured to make her stunning garments, or the way she'd looked at me as if I would make a tasty snack. And I tried not to think of Ellion, and the way he stirred something deep within me when he was close.

I had wanted to kiss him too. For someone who had never harbored the slightest romantic feeling for anyone before, this was more than confusing. I liked them both. Conor was gentle and sweet, he made me laugh and, when I was with him, I could almost forget that I was in the faery realm. He anchored me and with him my feet remained safely on solid ground. But Ellion was unyielding darkness and danger, mystery and magic. He untethered me from my existence, laid adventure and possibility before me. With him, I felt strangely free.

By the time I found my way back to the barn, I was

relieved to have nothing but nettles for company. They didn't leave me feeling uncertain or confused. Among them I could breathe, be entirely myself, and I faced the sight before me with a determined sigh.

"Right," I said to the plants. "We have a job to do. I'm going to try my best, but I'll need your help. We are going to make the king the most incredible garment he's ever had, and we're going to do it together."

My little speech was met with silence. I nodded. "Ready?"

Rolling my sleeves up, I set to work. The first thing I needed to do was bring some sort of order to this chaos. The day was warm and dry, and I began by dragging the nettles outside. All of them. It was slow, repetitive work, but I appreciated the distraction it gave me. For several glorious hours I didn't think about Conor or Ellion.

It was good to have a sense of purpose, just like I'd had when I cut nettles in the moonlight. It almost hadn't mattered whether I could succeed. I simply had to believe it was possible. And truthfully, it made me feel at home. I was used to working hard, tending to the animals and the vegetable patches. Boredom set in quickly without something to occupy me, and with boredom came time to reflect. Time to miss what I'd left behind. Time to fear for my grandma and whether she still lived.

I couldn't think about her too much or I would crumble to pieces. And this wasn't the place to fall apart. This was the place to concentrate obsessively on moving nettle stalks.

While the sun and moons danced their endless chase, I remained devoted to my task. Once all the nettles were moved out of the barn, I began gathering them into small bundles, using straw from the stables to hold them together. The unkind ridges of the leaves cut my fingers more than once, but I barely noticed, I was so busy with my plan. With the nettles in neat bunches, I was able to stack them back in the barn so even though I was surrounded I could actually move.

When that was done, it was time to start removing the flowers and stripping the leaves.

The flowers were simple enough to pick, and I collected them to press later. The leaves were a different matter. I quickly learned how *not* to do it. At first, I plucked them off one by one, like I used to when harvesting to make a soup from them, but I soon realized that would take me forever—and even if Locryn had frozen time back home, I knew I didn't have that long. I tried using my penknife to scrape them from the stalk, but the blade was too sharp for the fragile stems, and I only succeeded in damaging them.

This did at least teach me an important thing—that the fibers Beattie had spoken of were inside the stalks. That would be my next step, to extract them. But they were wet and sticky, covered in a kind of gum. How I was supposed to do anything with them, I had no idea.

That was a challenge for another day. First things first—the leaves.

The most efficient way was to hold the stem at the base in one hand, and then run my hand upwards, separating the leaves as I went. This would have worked brilliantly at home, where the only thing that could hurt were the poisonous hairs on the stalk that I was immune to. But here the serrated edges of the leaves made it almost impossible. I pushed through the pain of a thousand small cuts to start with, but after several hours I'd had enough. There had to be a better way.

I stepped into the gloom of the barn. "Ellion?" I spoke to the shadows. "If you can hear me, do you have a scrap of leather I can borrow?"

No reply came. It had been worth a try. But as I turned to go back outside, a voice sounded behind me.

"You seem to be under some illusion that you can summon me whenever you wish. Unless your name is Locryn, I do not answer to you."

I smiled sweetly as I faced him. "Then thank you for showing up so quickly."

Ellion regarded me with a combination of weariness and irritation. He held up a wineskin. "Is this suitable for what you require?"

"Perfect, thank you," I said. If I unpicked the stitching, I could use it as a cloth and a barrier between my hand and the stem. As I reached to take it from him he noticed my bloodied hands, and concern flickered in his eyes.

"You're hurt."

"I'm fine," I assured him. "Blame the nettles."

He cast his gaze about the barn, noting the bundles piled high. "You've been busy."

"Beattie gave me some guidance," I said, and if Conor had looked horrified at that revelation, it was nothing to Ellion's reaction.

"Would you like to explain to me how you're still breathing?"

"Funny," I said, folding my arms, "she asked me to consider the same thing."

Ellion's jaw clenched, and I wished he would talk to me, share what was going on in that mysterious mind of his.

"She also suggested I didn't go through with what the king has asked. She was very cryptic and kept muttering about whether he had found a way and could it be done. Would you like to shed any light on that for me?"

Ellion met my eyes, and I saw his conflict. He wanted to help me but was bound in servitude to say nothing more. I was going to have to work this out for myself.

"Okay, let's think. Beattie let me live because she wants to see if I can succeed," I speculated aloud. "She said turning nettles to cloth has never been done before and I think her interest in her craft outweighed her desire to kill me." I looked at Ellion and his neutral expression told me all I needed to know. If I had been wrong, he wouldn't have been able to refrain from gloating. "She said nettles were forbidden plants here, that no one could pick them. You didn't think I'd be able to either, nor did the king. I succeeded by overcoming the protective enchantment on them—"

A realization hit me and I gasped. "Locryn is trying to harness their power, isn't he? That's what Beattie was talking about. He doesn't want a fashion garment from me, but something that offers him protection. But from what?"

Ellion glanced behind him. "I have to go," he said, and I understood he'd heard his name through the shadows. He was being summoned. "You should heed Beattie's warning," he added as he walked away. "Are you sure you want to continue down this path? Would it be so bad to remain here and forget your tasks?"

There was something in the tone of his voice, a hint of longing that made my chest ache. In his own way, Ellion was asking me to stay. And the fact I forgot to breathe suggested part of me wanted to accept.

"My grandmother needs me." My words sounded like an apology.

He nodded before disappearing into the shadows. It was as though he'd taken all light and air with him, I couldn't move, couldn't speak. My chest seemed to have shrunk, not allowing enough space for my lungs to expand, or my heart to beat. Was this what it was to care for someone, to love someone? Why did people crave this? It *hurt*.

And I finally understood the king. He loved his queen and he was suffering. Whatever he wanted this garment for, it was all to do with Keita, the woman who preoccupied his every thought and desire.

He was trying to return to her.

# SIXTEEN

It didn't take me long to realize I'd wasted time moving the nettles out and bundling them before stripping the leaves. I should have done it all at once, but this was nothing if not a steep learning curve.

Now I had to undo the bundles, strip the leaves, and re-bundle the bare stalks, which was frustrating, but I tried to comfort myself that it delayed having to work out the next stage of the process.

My vague plan was to go back to the market and hope that some of the other stall-holders were more willing to tell me their secrets than Beattie had been, but I was running low on sherbets and wasn't convinced I'd be successful. Everyone here seemed to prefer to keep their distance from the nettles.

For now, there were leaves to strip. It was a laborious process, but the only way to finish was to keep going, no matter what.

Of course, there was also the question of whether I should even be doing this at all. I had no idea what Locryn's motives might be to find his way back to his queen. Was it reconciliation he sought? Or revenge?

The truth was, that for all the warnings, all the doubts, I had to see the deal through, for Grandma's sake. And if I was completely honest with myself, I was intrigued by the process, enjoyed working with the nettles. In fact, sitting outside my barn in the meadow, surrounded by my favorite plant, I was perfectly content.

I was humming happily to myself on a cloudy morning, resting flowers between nettle leaves before placing them under the weight of stones, when someone cleared their throat, and I looked up to see Conor approaching, a plate of food in his hands.

"Hello," he said.

I paused in my work, not realizing how much I'd missed him until now. How many days had it been since I'd last seen him? I couldn't remember and, with a pang of guilt, realized I'd not kept my promise to him about eating or sleeping.

He studied the pile of leaves on the ground and the heap of stems I'd already stripped. "You've been hard at work," he said.

"There's a lot to do."

Conor came closer and held out the dish of roasted vegetables. "Thought you might be hungry." He gave me his most lopsided smile.

I patted the ground beside me, inviting him to sit down while I thanked him for the food. The carrot-like vegetable, whatever it was, smelled like honey and I groaned with delight at my first mouthful. "That tastes good," I said, and gobbled the rest far faster than was socially acceptable.

"I should go," Conor said when I had finished. "Before Morcan notices I've slipped away."

"You've just got here," I said, not wanting him to leave. "How are you? How are the horses?"

"The horses are well."

When he said nothing more, I pressed, 'And you?"

He stared at the ground. "I'm all right. I've been thinking about home a lot. Haven't had anyone to distract me." He attempted a grin, but it didn't reach his eyes. "It's hard to know when I came here, but sometimes I sense I'm reaching some sort of anniversary, and my thoughts find their way back to that day more quickly."

"When you came through the hawthorn trees?"

He nodded. "I wish I could have introduced you to my mam." His voice was soft. "She would have liked you."

"Tell me about her," I said, shuffling closer to him. "Did she look like you?"

"Nah, I took after my da. She was fairer, bonny. And tiny. How she managed to carry six of us, I'll never know."

"You had brothers and sisters?"

"I was the youngest," he said. "Two sisters and three brothers. I . . ." His voice broke. "I can't remember their names anymore."

I slipped my arm through his and squeezed.

"The day I came here, I was having some rare time with my mam. Just the two of us. We were playing, laughing. Taking it in turns to hide. I was looking for her when I saw the trees. Thought I heard her voice. I would have followed her anywhere."

A tear spilled down his cheek.

"It haunts me, Nettle," he whispered. "The thought of her searching for me, screaming, panicking. She loved me, I know that much. As other memories fade, that doesn't. How did she carry on, not knowing what happened to me? What did she tell my da? My brothers and sisters?"

I rested my head on his shoulder, wishing I could ease his pain, but knowing I couldn't.

"What kind of son am I that I never found a way back to my mam? That I couldn't let her know I was alive, that I was all right?"

"It wasn't your fault," I said.

Conor moved slightly away from a discarded nettle leaf, our knees brushing. "Sometimes, I wonder what if I've made that all up? What if none of that memory is real? The faeries could easily have planted it in my head to upset me. They love making us see things that aren't really there. How can I trust any of it?"

"Are the memories here?" I asked, placing my hand gently on his head. "Or are they here?" And I moved to press my hand against his chest, feeling his heart beating through his clothes.

Our eyes met and Conor slowly smiled. "There."

"Then they're real," I said simply.

My own heart was beating too fast. I was still touching him, but neither of us moved and I didn't want to be the one to break the spell.

"I gave up for a long time," he said. "Did what I had to in order to survive. But then you arrived and reminded me who I was." He reached to extract some foliage from my hair. "All you've told me about our world has made me yearn for it once more. I want to return there and see how big it has grown. I want to visit your home on the hill and sit in the sunshine with you." We both briefly lost ourselves in that dream, but when he spoke again, his voice had hardened. "It will never happen though. I cannot ever leave this place, the faeries have seen to that."

Oddly, I wanted to defend them, say they weren't all bad. That Ellion wasn't, at least. But I couldn't say that without sharing how the shadow faery made my pulse race which wasn't something I wanted to tell the boy who made my heart flutter. This was horribly unfamiliar territory and I had no compass with which to navigate.

It was safer to change the subject. "What if your task isn't impossible? What if it's just not something you can achieve alone?"

Conor looked at me. "What do you mean?"

"Well, I've had plenty of help with my tasks. From you, Gammi, Beattie. Has anyone ever helped you?"

His brow creased. "No. Who's going to want to help me waste hours transporting straw from one cursed barn to another?"

"I think I might be able to spare some time," I teased. "The tasks Locryn sets aren't impossible. Though he's rigged the game for sure, maybe if we work together, we can succeed."

Conor's expression turned from dubious to hopeful. "You don't think that would break the rules of the deal?"

"Did you ever agree to completing the task alone?"

He shook his head. "No, that wasn't part of the agreement."

"Then we should be fine."

Conor smiled. "What are we waiting for?"

We did wait though until the Night Riders had gone out on patrol and Morcan had left to attend the ball. Conor and I met at the barn. He hadn't been joking, it was full of straw from floor to ceiling.

"Right, are you ready?" I asked him.

"It's not going to work," he replied dismally, as I banged the wooden legs of my barrow onto the ground.

"None of that attitude," I chided. "Come on, are you with me or not?"

We had decided the best place to start was to see whether Conor hadn't been fast enough on his own to beat the enchantment. Together we would be much speedier.

"With you." He grabbed a handful of straw and threw it into his barrow.

Full of energy for our new quest, we ran beneath the waxing moons, grateful for their glow that guided our way from barn to barn. The noise of the night market and music from the palace were faint echoes as we fought to defy the faery magic.

Steadily we made progress, and when the first barn was nearly empty, I abandoned my barrow and grabbed a broom to sweep the stray stalks into a pile, so that nothing would get missed.

When every wisp was loaded into the barrow, Conor sprinted with it toward the other barn, while I waited to see if we'd done enough.

The barn remained empty. I stood, holding my breath, willing us to have succeeded, and when I heard Conor shout that he had delivered the last barrow load, I could barely believe I continued to stand in a strawless barn. Had we done it? Had we really moved it all?

Conor was running back, and I stepped out to greet him, hardly daring to speak the words out loud, my expression saying everything.

"Is it empty?" he asked in disbelief.

I nodded, turning to reveal our victory, only for my hopes to be smashed to pieces.

In the seconds I'd been out of the barn, it had refilled. Conor stopped abruptly at my side. He said nothing.

"I'm sorry," I said. "It was empty. I don't understand."

It was a moment more before he spoke. "It's all right. I didn't really expect it to work anyway."

"We have to try again," I said, stubbornly.

"There's no point." I had never heard him sound so defeated.

"Tomorrow," I said firmly. "We'll try something different, okay? I'm not ready to give up, nor should you be."

In the end he agreed, but after he left to snatch some rest before the Night Riders returned, I traipsed back to my own barn, exhausted and despondent.

Perhaps it had been foolish to offer to help Conor. But he was my friend, I cared about him. How could I not try?

I was intending to take a nap of my own when I became acutely aware that I wasn't alone anymore.

"What are you doing?" Ellion asked from the shadows.

"Trying to sleep. What about you?"

"I've come to warn you," he said, and there was something in his tone of voice that made me realize he wasn't here of his own volition.

"Oh really? About what?"

Ellion's face was hidden by shadows, so I couldn't read his expression. "You should focus on your own task."

Anger flared. "Are you spying on me?"

Ignoring me, Ellion continued. "The king didn't intend for tasks to be shared."

"Then he should have been more specific," I spat. "I can't believe you. Do you report back to Locryn about everything?"

Ellion stepped toward me, out of the shadows, and his fierceness caught me off guard—which was saying something, given that he was always intense.

"You know what I am, who I serve," he said. "I cannot escape that any more than you can."

"So you watch me from the shadows and tell Locryn what you see?" When I saw shame in his eyes, my anger grew. "Does he know that you spy on him too? Are you loyal to anyone?"

Ellion's eyes searched mine, and perhaps he saw something there he didn't expect, because the atmosphere shifted between us, and I was possessed by an unnerving need to press my lips to his. I briefly considered that he might have bewitched me, but then I saw the longing and confusion in his own face and realized he'd felt the same thing.

We both took a step backwards, retreating to more familiar anger.

"Heed my words," Ellion said. "Stop trying to help the stable boy."

"Or what?" I folded my arms defiantly.

His gaze ran across my jaw and down my neck before he forced it back to my eye level. "Or you'll regret it." And in a smooth sweep, he returned to the shadows and disappeared, leaving me furious—and even worse, disappointed.

---

The next night I met Conor with renewed determination.

"I've had an idea," I said, approaching him with almost a spring in my step. "I can't believe I didn't think about it sooner." I pulled the horseshoe from my pocket.

Conor stared at it. "I thought that was in your enchanted sack."

"It was, I'd completely forgotten about it. I don't need the sack anymore, so it can break the enchantment for you instead."

"You think that will work?" He sounded doubtful.

"We know iron repels their magic. It's worth a try."

I could tell how dangerously low his reserves of hope were. The last thing I wanted was to deplete them entirely. But I truly thought this had a good chance of succeeding.

"All right." He gave in, accepting I wasn't to be dissuaded. "Let's load the barrows."

We set to work quickly, and though we were both tired, we made good progress transferring the straw.

From time to time, I glanced at the horseshoe, which I'd placed on the ground, and as the barn cleared, I nudged it into the middle of the space. It had to work, it just had to. There had to be a way home for Conor. A happy ending to his story.

Perhaps it wasn't only his hope reserves that were low.

The night drew on, the crows cawing loudly, and when the stalks were all transferred to the other barn, I waited.

By the time Conor returned to my side, hot tears burned my cheeks.

"I'm so sorry," I said, as he took in the sight. The barn was full again—all apart from the space around the horseshoe, as if it was the center of a meteor crater. "I don't think it's powerful enough for such a big space."

I thought he might deflate in the face of such disappointment, but he tensed. "I should have known better than to get my hopes up," he said.

"I'm sorry," I repeated and tried to take his hand in mine. He pulled it away.

Knowing I deserved that, I stepped into the barn and picked up the horseshoe, tucking it into my pocket. As I left, the remainder of the straw billowed back, removing any hint of victory.

Ellion was waiting for me when I returned to my nettles. He was the last person I wanted to see, even if he was dressed elaborately, as though he had come straight from the ball, his pants sparkling with diamonds, shadows spun across his chest and arms like the inkiest tattoos.

He saw my fury and folded his arms. "I did warn you."

I stormed toward him. "Why? Why won't you let us win?"

"You know that you can, just that it's very hard."

"I am sick of you and your technicalities," I shouted, all my fury and weariness coming to a head. "It's not fair to give people hope and dangle it like an ever-out-of-reach carrot."

My anger seemed to bounce off Ellion, who remained impassive. "I told you to focus on your own task."

"Go away, Ellion."

I pushed past him into the barn, wanting to tuck myself up and sleep forever, forget the disappointment on Conor's face.

But Ellion followed and watched me from the doorway.

"The stable boy made a mistake early on," he said.

"What do you mean?"

"On his first attempt to complete his task, he dropped some straw between the barns, and it blew away on the wind. Therefore, he cannot move all the straw from one barn to the other."

I stared at Ellion in horror. "You mean he's already failed? All this time, no matter what he does, he can't succeed?"

Ellion said nothing.

"You're evil," I whispered. "You faeries. Tricking people like this, it's cruel. Soulless."

"I did warn you that you would regret it," Ellion said.

"There's nothing he can do then," I said. "There's no way he can ever go home."

"The chances were slim anyway."

"Leave me alone," I said, unable to bear the sight of him or any other faery right now. This time, he knew not to argue with me and vanished into the shadows. The moment he was gone, I burst into tears. Because the truth was, I wasn't angry with him. He hadn't been the one to raise Conor's hopes. No, that was me, and I couldn't forgive myself.

# SEVENTEEN

That night I dreamed I was back in the white forest again. I followed the sound of silver bells until I saw the girl in the distance. The one who looked like me. She wasn't crying this time though — she was happy. Her smile was a bright flame, and I the moth drawn to it. The dream girl was picking nettles, but not with a knife. She was doing it with her bare hands and gathering them in her apron.

"You like nettles too?" I asked, which seemed silly because she was me. Wasn't she?

The mist swirled and the scene changed. Now I was watching the dream version of myself sitting in a pool of moonlight, running her hands up the stalks, removing the leaves. She sang to herself — or was it to the nettles — as she gently bundled the leafless stems together and laid them on the ground in neat rows.

I blinked and realized time had passed. The bundles had turned from fresh green stalks to brown, as though they were rotting. The girl took a single stem and created a slit in the woody pith with her nail, peeling it away from the fibers within. I wanted to see more and stepped nearer, but the mist closed in, blurring my vision.

*Nettle*, the voice called. *Nettle*.

I woke, my breathing fast and uneven. Around me I could hear my name being murmured, as if the nettles themselves were talking to me.

"Are you trying to tell me what to do?" I asked as the sound faded.

Was it possible? Could plants really be talking to me in my sleep? It sounded ridiculous, but wasn't everything in this place?

Straight away I set to work, copying what I'd seen myself doing in the dream and laid the bare stems in bundles on the ground, hoping that the nettles truly were guiding me.

I tried not to think about Conor. How could I face him again, knowing his fate had been sealed long ago, and he could never return to the human world? I had been arrogant, thought because I had made some progress with my task, that I knew better than everyone else, when I should have left things alone.

When Ellion appeared, I ignored him. I was in no mood to talk. But he didn't leave. Eventually, he broke the silence. "You know, I was trying to help you," he said. "You were wasting time with the stable boy when you have your own tasks to complete."

"You can tell the king I'm going as fast as I can. I know he's anxious to get his precious garment."

"I was thinking of you," he said. "I know your grandmother's wellbeing is of the utmost importance. I didn't wish for you to be sidetracked."

His words made me stop what I was doing, and at last I looked at him. He appeared genuine and I lost the desire to fight with him.

"Well, I'm back at work, as you can see," I said wearily.

"Possibly not for long," he said. "I'm here with a message for you. Lassila Lindelburr has sent word that you are to attend on her as a matter of urgency. Apparently Miss Marigold is unwell."

"What's wrong, do you know?"

"I have given you the message in its entirety."

"Okay, I'd better hurry. Oh, I don't have one of those stick things to take me there and the route never seems quite the same."

Ellion hesitated before saying, "I could take you there through the shadows, if you wish."

"You would do that?" It was unlike Ellion to make such an offer. The only time he'd done it before was when I'd strayed into Locryn's private chamber and he urgently needed to remove me.

"I believe I would." Ellion gave me that rarest of things. A smile.

While it was probably only because he was trying to restore peace between us, I appreciated his help. It would save me a lot of time. And I wanted peace again too.

Ellion held out his hand and I took it. He pulled me close and practically danced me into the shadows.

I was dizzy when he released me and it had nothing to do with the swift traveling through darkness. But when I glanced to see if he was similarly affected by our close proximity, he was regarding me with a strange expression, as if he had just heard the most troubling news.

"What?" I asked, feeling I'd missed something important.

He simply gestured to the house before us. "You're expected." Then he was gone without so much as a goodbye. Clearly his goodwill wasn't going to last that long.

There wasn't time to worry about Ellion though, and I hurried to knock on the painted door.

"Thank goodness you're here," Nyla said, beckoning me in. "Miss Marigold is in quite a state."

She escorted me through to the drawing room, where Marigold lay on the couch, and Lassila stood over her looking remarkably unconcerned. In fact, she looked bored.

"I came as quickly as I could," I said, rushing to Marigold's side and taking her hand. "Whatever is wrong?"

Lassila rolled her eyes. "Absolutely nothing of consequence."

Marigold gasped indignantly. "How can you say such a thing?" But she sat up with a smile and squeezed my hand. "I'm thrilled you came." Then she pouted. "Where have you been?"

I stared at her, confused. "I don't understand, I thought you were ill?"

"I have been wretched!" she insisted. "Waiting for you to visit, searching for you at the balls. You disappeared on me."

"I barely noticed," Lassila said, in case I should make the mistake of thinking she cared.

Ignoring her, I moved to sit beside Marigold. "I'm sorry, I've been busy. It wasn't my intention to neglect you."

She pursed her lips, and then gave a little jump that sent her curls bouncing. "In that case, you are forgiven. Now tell me you're coming to the ball tonight."

I thought of my nettles lying on the ground to rot. I probably did have time while nature took its course. "If it would make you happy," I agreed. If she noticed my lack of enthusiasm, it didn't show.

"I will need you, for I am expecting Ketter Bonberry to propose." Her rosy cheeks reddened further.

"That's wonderful," I said, noting that Lassila didn't seem to share my sentiments.

"He declared his love at the last ball, it was so romantic. We're going to live in his beautiful home, and Lassila's going to come and stay with us, aren't you?"

Lassila said nothing, but Marigold was too busy filling me in on the details to notice.

I spent the rest of the afternoon with them, listening to Marigold's enthusiastic, but endless, stories of what Ketter had said, and what Ketter had done. A small part of me yearned to be similarly the object of someone's affection, but the realization that I didn't know whether I wanted that someone to be Conor or Ellion put pay to that. What did it matter? There was no future with either of them. Once this cloth was made, I would receive my final task and upon completing it, would return to my life on the hill. And Conor and Ellion would both belong to a weird and wonderful dream that would fade over time.

When Nyla came to dress us for the ball, Marigold chose a particularly lacy gown, especially for the occasion. I was disconcerted when she handed me a package.

"This is for you," she said. "I thought you deserved something of your own for such a special evening."

"You're so kind," I said, taking it from her. Carefully unwrapping the paper, I gasped when I saw what was inside and shook the dress out before me. At first sight, the material appeared black, but when it moved in the light, it shimmered purple and blue. The straps were made of black rose petals and the skirt had silver taffeta flowing over it, which gleamed like a midnight waterfall. "It's beautiful," I gasped. "Thank you so much."

"Lassila picked it," Marigold said. "She thought it would suit you."

Such a gesture was hard to believe. I turned to the impenetrable faery and smiled. "Thank you, you chose perfectly."

Lassila inclined her head. "Let us see how it looks."

Nyla helped me into it and tied the laces at the back, before attaching my gauze wings.

"I know you prefer to have bare feet," Marigold said, 'but these shoes spoke to me, told me you'd admired them." And she handed me the pair I'd seen in the shop the day I'd first met her, the ones made of twilight rose petals.

"They spoke to you?" I asked, raising an eyebrow.

"Why of course they did," she said, as if it was a stupid question. "How else would I know what to get you?"

Despite them looking several sizes too big, as I slipped into the shoes, they molded to fit my feet. They were possibly the most comfortable things I had ever worn.

"And your mask matches," Marigold said with great satisfaction, passing it to me. "Have we not done a faultless job dressing you?"

I took it gratefully. "You really have."

"Here," Lassila said, passing me a goblet. "Drink this."

I stared at it suspiciously. "What is it?"

Lassila laughed. "You are always so mistrustful. Something to celebrate the night ahead." She passed a goblet to Marigold before taking another for herself.

"A toast. To my beloved Marigold and to dreams coming true."

"To dreams coming true," Marigold and I parroted back, and, knowing to refuse would be rude, I brought the bubbling golden liquid to my lips. A little couldn't hurt.

A single sip fizzed on my tongue with such sweetness I thought I would never wish to drink again unless it was this. All my concerns melted away, and serenity enveloped me.

"To the ball," Lassila said, ushering me and Marigold out of the door. I barely needed any encouragement.

I was ready to dance forever.

# EIGHTEEN

The ballroom had never looked so magnificent.

As we walked down the spiral staircase, it seemed to me that the masked faeries wore dresses beyond anything I could dream. They spun around the ballroom in the arms of even more devastatingly handsome partners than usual. The music flowed over me like a summer breeze.

The second we reached the room, the desire to dance was impossible to ignore.

"Go!" Lassila's lips twitched. "I will help Marigold find Ketter. You must enjoy yourself."

"I don't know any of the steps," I protested, but Lassila was waving someone over.

She leaned close to me. "Abandon your inhibitions," she murmured. "Tonight, you are not bound by any limits, so do not resist."

And then a faery in a gown of spun gold took my hand and whisked me with her onto the dance floor.

My head was light, and my feet moved as if floating above the ground. Together the stranger and I whirled around the ballroom, and I closed my eyes in sheer bliss. When I opened them, the faery was looking at me with undisguised longing and somewhere deep inside a warning scratched within me, but then the music swept the worry away, and I smiled coyly.

Never before had I felt so beautiful, so desirable, so important. I commanded this room, belonged in it, and, after a lifetime of hiding in the shadows, I relished every moment.

Giddy with delight, I twirled and dipped, breathing the music like air, and then the stranger released me, so that I danced alone, my head tipped back as I spun on the spot. I never wanted this to end, this ecstasy.

Who knows how long I danced before an unpleasant nausea began to creep up my throat and I wobbled, unsteady on my feet. I tried to slow down, but my feet wouldn't let me, turning and tapping, though the music no longer sounded quite as mesmerizing. In fact, it was discordant and grating. My head began to thrum, and when I glanced about, I caught glimpses of the faeries' faces. Gone was their beauty, in its place fangs and dark pits for eyes. When I blinked, everything was back to normal, but I no longer felt the giddy euphoria. I wanted to leave.

Fighting against the blur of my vision, I staggered off the dance floor, searching for the door, but everything was too bright, too loud. I couldn't stand still, and I realized my shoes were enchanted. I tried to kick them off, but they wouldn't budge, and I cursed myself for accepting Marigold's gift. I had to practically contort myself to bend and rip them from my feet, and once I had, I was mercifully able to stop moving. The skin on my soles was torn, blood smeared everywhere, and I winced as I tried to touch them.

What had been in the drink Lassila had given me? Why had she tricked me and Marigold? Had she thought such wild abandon would be fun?

My eyes searched among the dancing faeries and the few humans for either Marigold or Lassila. But as I watched the revellers the same thing happened as before. The faeries would turn, and I would see their true appearance beneath the glamours, skulls void of flesh, soulless caverns where eyes should be. Then they would spin again and beauty and perfection were restored. But I had seen it, the grim, rotting heart of this place that they concealed so heavily with magic to make it seem otherwise.

Another wave of sickness washed over me, and I stumbled painfully toward the far corner where Ellion had once taken me. I had never wanted to see him so badly, needed to cling to him like a rock in the stormiest of waters. This place was a dark dream and even from his shadows, I knew Ellion would lead me back to the light.

But when I reached the gap between the hedgerow walls, it wasn't the same as before. It was colder, damper. A chill spread up my arms.

"Ellion?" I whispered, hoping he would hear me. I kept walking, though every step was agony and the shadows grew deeper. The music from the ballroom gave way to a different tune. It sounded as though it was played by a grieving orchestra, each note a lament. Tears pooled in my eyes as I moved toward it.

I came to an abrupt halt. I had reached another ballroom, and as much as the previous dance floor was awash with giddy energy, this was shrouded in gloom.

The dancers were dressed in suits and gowns of drab grey, adorned with cobwebs and dust. Their hair was white, their skin sallow, and they moved slowly to an eerie waltz. No one spoke, no one laughed. They moved as if they were lifeless dolls, controlled by an unseen faery puppeteer.

Even the room was grey—a pale imitation of the faery land I'd come to know. A trestle table was covered in platters of moldering food, draped in web and maggots. Surprisingly, I couldn't smell it—only a musty dampness that made me think of death.

Keeping to the side of the room, I wandered around, observing the dancers, realizing with horror that they were all humans. I approached a young girl in what looked like a servant's outfit from the early twentieth century.

"Hello? Can you hear me?"

She stared through me as if I wasn't there, not stopping her dancing.

"What are you doing here?" I asked, pressing my hand to hers and gasping. It was ice cold. "Who are you?"

"Someone neither alive nor dead."

The sound of his voice was a welcome relief. I turned to face Ellion, dressed entirely in black as always, though his clothes shimmered with starlight, his magnificent wings stretched wide. He was watching me with his usual serious expression.

"What is this place?" I asked. "Who are they?"

"They are the dream-walkers."

"They're asleep?" I glanced back at the young girl, whose eyes were very definitely open, even if they did not see.

"In a sense. They're humans who came to this realm by theft or deception, and realized too late the burden of what they would consider immortality. They're the souls who sought an audience with the king, or at times, the queen, and begged for release. Or the discarded servants of faeries who found humans were inefficient once their worn spirits no longer matched their glamoured bodies. They are sent here, into this limbo, forced into an endless dance, cursed never to stop."

"That's awful, it's too cruel," I whispered. "Can we help them?"

Ellion shook his head. "They are trapped here forever. They cannot be saved."

I looked at him in despair. My head ached from the fading enchantment, my feet stung from dancing, but my discomfort couldn't compare to what these dream-walkers had to endure. Is this what would become of Conor eventually? Would Marigold find herself here when Lassila and Ketter grew weary of her? And what about me? If I failed in my tasks, would I beg for mercy only to be imprisoned here?

Moving away from the dancers, I tiptoed toward Ellion.

"You called for me."

My eyes filled with tears. "I was afraid. Lassila practically drugged me, and then I felt lost." I hesitated. "Sometimes, in the corner of my eye, things appear different here. Beautiful shops are just ruins. Gorgeous faeries are monsters. I have never known a place so dangerous, so deceptive. So, tell me, why do I sometimes find myself wanting to stay?"

He was watching me keenly, his jaw rigid. "You can see through glamours."

I nodded, wondering why I somehow felt ashamed at such an admission. And then I realized. I was basically telling him he was a monster beneath his beauty.

"Will you take me home?" I asked, and he nodded, pulling me into his arms.

I sensed we were back in my barn before I opened my eyes. I didn't want to move away from him, but to linger was a danger of its own.

I stepped backwards and smiled. "I didn't mean to offend you," I said.

"What, when you implied my incredible good looks were an illusion?"

I opened my mouth to object, but realized he was teasing. "To be fair," I said, "you've never appeared differently to me when I've glanced away."

"That's because I'm a shadow faery and we have no need of cheap glamours. We are able to appear as we see ourselves."

"We? How many of you are there?"

He drew a breath. "Only two that I know of. One lives far away from here."

"And the other?"

Ellion sighed, as though he carried the weight of many worlds. "You once asked me what I did to become a changeling."

I noted the change of conversation, but I was too eager to hear the rest of this story to care.

"I was neither old and desperate to die, nor fascinated by your world and eager to visit. I was following orders."

That was not what I had been expecting him to say. "I don't understand."

"Locryn had a brother," Ellion explained. "A younger and far more foolish faery called Alamond, who without any responsibility to his kingdom enjoyed frivolities even more than most. He was constantly inebriated and his mood frequently foul. A spoiled wretch of a man. I disliked him immensely. One day he got into a fight with another faery and killed him." Ellion paused to look at me. "You understand the immensity of that? Faeries are not immortal, and their long lives can be ended instantly by murder. It is the worst crime a faery can commit, to take the life of another without the king's permission. The punishment is banishment in the form of a changeling child. And Locryn couldn't bring himself to do that to his brother, no matter his crime."

"So he framed you?" I asked in horror.

Ellion smiled sadly. "No. He is the king, he simply had to order me to take the blame for Alamond. He knew I would follow orders, even though I had no expectation of surviving."

That, right there, was the essence of Ellion. He would take the punishment for another simply out of loyalty.

"But you did," I said softly. "How?"

"It's not impossible for a changeling to live in the human realm, given the right circumstances. Luck plays a huge part. I was swapped with the babe of a hunter who lived in the forest. He always suspected what I truly was, but raised me and kept me safe, but most importantly, kept me close to the veil between worlds. That's what a changeling needs most, to be near the energy of their own kingdom. Stray too far from it and they would quickly fade away."

"What happened to the child you were switched with?"

"Given to the family of the deceased as compensation. He still works in their kitchens, I believe."

I strongly suspected that Ellion watched over him from the shadows more than he'd admit. "How long were you in my world?"

"Seven years, and here is the most important thing— unlike most, I retained all my faery memories. I wanted to return home, and with my faery knowledge, knew how to recognize a portal between the worlds. I found a faery ring, stepped inside the circle of toadstools, and found myself back here. I thought Locryn would be thrilled to see me, would welcome me back with open arms, after the sacrifice I had made for him."

"Instead you found yourself alone," I whispered.

He scoffed. "I underestimated his hatred for humans, how he now saw me as something less than I was before. The thing is, he's as obsessed with humans as any other faery. Do you think faeries like Lord Lindelburr bring human babies here because they care? Or mischievous faeries trick them to step through portals because they actually want to spend time with them? They are momentarily intrigued by humans before they tire of them. But they wouldn't feel that way if they spent a fraction of time in the human world, as I did. Humans are not objects of fascination, they are not curiosities for us to play with. Our realms should remain separate—humans don't belong here, we don't belong there. It's best to accept it once and for all."

We fell silent, before Ellion shuffled awkwardly. "You should rest. You have work to do."

"I can't do anything in this," I said, gesturing to my dress. "I might have to pay Marigold a visit to free me from it."

"Here," he said, taking my elbow, pulling me close and moving behind me. He untied my wings and dropped them to the floor. And then he began to unlace the many ribbons at the back of my dress.

His fingers grazed my skin and sparks flew through me. With each lace, he brushed against me, a soft caress that set me alight. I never wanted his touch to end.

"All done," he said, and his voice was low as he turned me round to face him.

I stared at him with true longing. "Sometimes I don't want to go home." The words spilled unbidden from my lips like a confession.

"Sometimes I don't want you to either." His face inched closer to mine and I closed my eyes in anticipation.

"What *do* you want?" I barely breathed the words.

"For you to wake up," he said softly.

"I am awake," I promised, wishing he would just kiss me already.

"Then answer me this. Who are you?"

The air around me grew suddenly cold. When I opened my eyes, he was gone.

# NINETEEN

I couldn't sleep. I lay awake until the sun rose, thinking of Conor and how he had already failed his task, of the dream-walkers in their perpetual torment, and tried very hard not to think of Ellion and the effect of his touch on me.

I had changed back into the dress that Marigold had given me long ago, preferring it to my old linen dress, which had become so filthy I kept it for only my messiest jobs. All that did was remind me that too often, when presented with a choice, I was drawn to the faery one, rather than the human.

With the remaining stem bundles left on the ground, there was little I could do but wait. I needed a distraction from my thoughts. To get out of here, to clear my head.

I hurried down to the yard.

As expected, the Night Riders had long returned, and Conor was finishing his morning chores. I waited until he set off with a full barrow toward the muck heap, hidden from sight beyond the stables, and hurried over to Pym.

She greeted me with a nicker as I opened the stall.

"I know you've had a long night already," I said to her. "But I need to breathe and I can't do it here. May I take you for a ride?"

She answered by lowering her front legs to give me a chance of climbing onto her high back. My own legs weren't long enough to reach the knots in her mane used by the Night Riders as stirrups, so I simply wound my fingers into the tresses I could reach, as she straightened up. I had to lie flat on her neck as she trotted out of the stable, to avoid being hit, and found my balance just before she broke into a canter. All I could do was stay on, letting Pym take me in the right direction as she thundered through the arch, away from the palace and into the town. There were a few stragglers on the road, who hurried out of our way and stared at us in astonishment. I paid them no heed. There was only me and Pym in the whole world, as she sped down the hillside, leaving behind the market and the cloud of confusion that surrounded me there.

When we reached open moorland, Pym wasted no time pressing into the gallop that had previously taken my breath away. I had been afraid then. Now . . . this was exhilarating! We were flying together across the moors and for a brief and wonderful moment, I could believe I had wings of my own. All thoughts were banished, all fears forgotten. There was only me, this powerful horse, and total freedom.

The forest loomed before me. The realm of Queen Keita. What would have happened if I'd made it there that first day, if the Night Riders hadn't caught me? The glimpse of the queen and her court in Locryn's mirror suggested it was a far better place than the moorland court, but I now knew better than to believe anything I saw. No doubt I would simply be bargaining for my freedom with a different monarch.

*Nettle.*

The voice enveloped me as the wind whipped up, both my hair and Pym's mane blowing wildly, and the horse reared in defiance.

The call was strong, the pull toward the forest immense. Was the queen summoning me? Or possibly the trees? I didn't care—against all reason, I wanted to go, and I would have, had Pym not circled and galloped against the wind, her head low as she carried me away from the hypnotic lure of the forest.

When we had broken free of the enchantment, I patted Pym on her neck. "Thank you," I breathed. Things could have ended very differently if not for the mare's quick thinking.

The ride back to the moorland court was calmer, as if Pym understood it was what I needed, and by the time we cantered back into the yard, I was wonderfully refreshed, and ready to face all that awaited me.

Conor was deep in an animated conversation with Morcan, and they both turned to gawp, as Pym came to a halt and I slipped from her back.

"Hi," I greeted them with a smile.

Neither of them returned it.

"Hi?" Conor shouted. "You stole Pym and that's all you have to say? Hi?"

Their anger caught me off guard. "I didn't steal her," I said defensively.

"Do you know how worried I've been?" Conor asked. "I had no idea where she was."

"You rode her." Morcan's low voice was far more menacing than Conor's spiky anger, and he stepped toward me, his eyes shining. "How? No one can ride these horses apart from the Night Riders and me."

"I'm not a bad rider," I said, glancing at Conor who eyed me in a way I didn't like. He hadn't been angry with me since I first arrived. "Plus, she did everything, I just held on really."

"No, I mean, how?"

"You're right, I should have asked permission," I apologized. "I'm sorry, I needed to clear my head."

"I'm not saying only the Night Riders are allowed to ride the horses, I'm telling you only they *can*. So I repeat, *how* did you ride one?" Morcan stared at me as if he'd never seen me before.

I looked at Conor for help, but he was clearly waiting for my answer too.

## Nettle

"I don't know," I said honestly. "I asked her if she would take me, and she did. I'm sorry," I repeated. "I'll settle her in her stable."

"No." Morcan was emphatic. "I forbid you to come here again, understand? I don't want you near my horses."

"She didn't mean any harm," Conor said, trying to reason with him.

Morcan ignored him and stepped up to me, so his face was in mine. "Who are you?"

I hesitated, confused by his wrath. "I'm me."

"Hmm." The sound was a growl. "You are keeping something secret, and I don't like it. Say your goodbyes and go."

When I nodded, he strode off, leaving me alone with Conor, who came to take Pym. I watched awkwardly while he put her back in her stall and waited for him to speak his mind. I knew he had something to say.

"That's not the first time someone's mentioned your secret," he said, as he bolted her stable door shut. "Is there something you want to share with me?"

I thought about the many secrets I was keeping from him—how I came to be here, his failed task, my tender moments with Ellion. I shook my head. "I don't know what he means."

Conor studied my face then sighed. "I don't believe you," he said, before adding, "but I do trust you. So whatever your reasons are for keeping things to yourself, that's fine with me."

My cheeks turned scarlet, as I nodded my thanks.

"Where did you and Pym go?" he asked, and I was relieved he was trying to lighten the mood.

"Out on the moors," I replied. "It was wonderful."

"I thought you might have been with your friend in town."

I frowned. "Marigold? Why?"

"Heard some chatter in town this morning, when I was looking for a missing horse. Apparently Ketter Bonberry proposed last night."

I clapped my hands. "Oh, that's amazing. Marigold was sure he was going to."

Conor wasn't smiling. "He proposed to Adlyn Thorncott."

My own smile faded. "Oh no. Poor Marigold. I should go to her." I started to leave, but then I turned back to him. "Are we okay?"

He nodded, and to my relief the smile he gave me was real. "We are. Now go, before Morcan catches you here."

I stepped forward to give him a swift hug and then hurried away toward the town before he could say anything more.

It was only when I reached the cobbled street that I remembered I didn't know the way.

"Help me out?" I asked the paths, knowing they could move about to lead me to Marigold's home if they chose to. I continued in the vague direction that I was sure the house was in, taking every twisting path and narrow street I could find. As I went along a shadowy alley, I tried to picture the house and the street, bringing to mind anything familiar to help me recognize it, and as if by magic, I was there.

Nyla opened the door before I knocked. "We weren't expecting you."

"I came to see Marigold, is she well?"

Nyla nodded, bemused as she gestured for me to go through, and I went into the drawing room, where Marigold was dancing on the leaves while Lassila played the piano.

"Nettle!" Marigold cried and danced toward me, taking my hands and spinning me around. "Isn't it a perfect day?"

"I didn't expect to find you in such high spirits," I said, utterly confused. "Are you all right?"

"Happy as a lark!" she proclaimed.

I glanced at Lassila, who abruptly stopped playing and rose to her feet. "Enough of this. Nettle, a word?" She nodded, curtly, to indicate she wished for us to leave the room.

"Of course," I said, a terrible feeling coming over me.

Lassila took me into another room, and as soon as the door was shut, I rounded on her. "What have you done?"

"Only what is best for Marigold," she replied.

I stared at her. "She loved Ketter! She wanted to marry him!"

"I couldn't allow that to happen," Lassila replied. "Marigold is mine."

"Yours?" I shook my head. "She loves you, Lassila, she believes you are a true friend. How could you?"

"I haven't harmed her," Lassila said, and anger flared in her eyes. "She danced happily all night and doesn't remember a thing about Ketter Bonberry. Neither should you."

"Well, I do, and while we're on the subject, I didn't appreciate being drugged by you."

There was no apology. "I did what I had to do. Ketter didn't deserve Marigold, she wouldn't have been happy. I love her too, Nettle, no matter what you may think. She is the closest thing I have to a daughter. I couldn't let her leave."

"That isn't love. Controlling someone isn't love. Lying to someone isn't love. Making them forget who they are isn't love. You are selfish, Lassila. I want no part in it."

I stormed out and marched into the drawing room, where Marigold looked at me in surprise.

"What's the matter?" she asked as I sat beside her.

"I want you to come back to the palace with me," I said, trying to contain my emotions. "You're not safe here."

Marigold laughed. "Not safe? This is my home." When she saw I wasn't laughing, she said, "Oh dear. Have I forgotten something silly again?"

I fixed her with my firmest gaze. "Lassila is lying to you. About a great many things. There's a lot she doesn't tell you and more that she makes you forget. I'm sorry, but it's the truth."

She took my hand in hers. "Nettle, it's all right. I know."

"What do you mean?" I asked, confused. I had never seen Marigold this serious before.

"I mean, I know that Lassila lies to me from time to time. She makes decisions for me, but it's all right. I trust her. She looks out for me, as a favor to Lord Lindelburr."

I couldn't quite believe it. How could she be so accepting of the deception? "It's not right. You don't belong here, Marigold. You're a human. Don't you want to go home to the world you're from?"

A sad smile played on her lips. "I don't remember anything about that place. I don't know what it means to be human, beyond what Lassila tells me. This is the only home I know, Nettle. Why would I want to leave?"

"Because you aren't free."

She leaned forward conspiratorially. "Who is?"

Our eyes met and what I saw there made me want to weep. But then Marigold blinked. "Oh, Nettle, how lovely to see you. I wasn't expecting you today, but I have such news. Lassila said we might take a trip soon, I wonder where we might go. Perhaps you could join us, wouldn't that be wonderful?"

Something inside me broke. This last enchantment had pushed her too far. There was only so much meddling a mind could endure and I knew that Marigold was wandering lost and alone inside hers.

I stood up and walked out of the room. When I left the house, I knew it was for the last time. I would never be coming back.

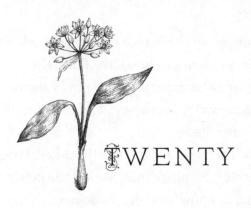

# TWENTY

For a while, I hid in my barn, avoiding faeries and humans alike.

Lassila's betrayal of Marigold had shaken me, and I mourned the loss of my friend and the life she had been denied.

I wanted to talk to Conor about it, but his hope was already hanging by a thread. And I couldn't talk to Ellion because I knew I would blame him, even though none of it was his fault. He was guilty simply for being a part of this place.

Time passed in the uncertain way it did here and I found a kind of peace in the rhythm of inspecting, turning, and checking my nettles. The sun was especially warm when I decided the stems had turned brown enough. They were the same color they had been in my dream, and so I picked one up and made a slit in the brittle woodiness, just as the dream version of me had. I ran my finger up the length of the stem, taking care around the nodes not to break the fibers. I wasn't entirely sure what I was expecting, but the fibers were dry, free from any gummy stickiness, and peeled easily away from the outer stem.

I shrieked with delight. It had actually worked, I had managed to extract the fibers from within the nettles. Now all I needed to know was what to do next.

Impatient for the moons to rise, I tried to nap, but I lay wide awake. It was frustrating how little I needed sleep here, especially when I was desperate to dream. All that happened was my mind wandered to dark places, where I feared I had taken too long, that this would be for nothing, that Grandma would be long dead and I would return to a lonely existence.

I spent two more turns of the moons busily extracting the fibers before sleep claimed me.

As always, I followed the voice whispering my name through the mist, until it led me to a glade, where the girl in the green dress sat surrounded by discarded dried stems and was rolling the inner fibers between her palms. When she had worked the bunches into a thick twine, she picked up a comb and scraped the handful of fibers across the blunt side, teasing out the softer fibers. It was slow and time-consuming, but she didn't seem to mind, humming to herself as she worked.

The mist closed in, concealing her from me, and when it dispersed once more, the girl was sitting at a spinning wheel, feeding threads of the extracted fibers into it, her foot pressing rhythmically against the pedal to keep the wheel turning. I edged closer, keen to learn more, and was shocked to see that the girl who looked oh-so-like me had a swollen belly, which she stroked affectionately from time to time.

While I considered what that could mean, the mist swirled again, and when it lifted the girl was standing at a loom, weaving the threads she had spun on the wheel. Her pregnancy was obvious, but all her previous happiness was gone, replaced with uncertainty. And as I watched, I wondered how I had ever thought she was me. We weren't that alike. But there was something, some connection, and I reached to touch her . . .

*Nettle.*

I woke with such a weight on my chest, I could barely breathe. The dream had shown me the next step in my process, but the emotion of the woman still clung to me. Who did I keep dreaming about? For so long, I'd assumed it was me, but now I was certain I was wrong. All this time, I'd been relying on her help and had forgotten she'd once asked for mine.

I would have to think on it before I next managed to sleep. Until then, the dream had shown me what to do next. But I didn't have a spinning wheel or a loom.

As the silver moon led night's charge, I paid Gammi another visit. She spotted me walking along the bustling streets.

"Been wondering when you would come and see old Gammi again," she said, grabbing my skirt and pulling me toward her stall. "Got anything for me?" She licked the drool running down her chin.

"That depends," I said. "Do you have anything for me?"

Gammi gestured to her wares. "The best of everything, what do you need? A thread to lead you to true love? Or to punish your enemy? What is it that fuels you, girl? Love or hate?"

I thought briefly of Ellion and wondered if it could be both simultaneously?

"Actually, I wondered if you have a spinning wheel I could purchase. Or a loom?"

Gammi spat on the ground. "I don't sell such things, only my threads. Why do you waste Gammi's time?"

"But you must use a wheel," I pressed. "To make your amazing threads."

"Of course I do, but mine is not for sale. You want such a thing, you have to take the same risk Gammi did."

"Risk?"

Gammi nodded. "The only one who sells what you seek is Gizler."

Gizler. The goblin who set traps in the forest to capture supplies for his horrifying store. Great.

"Would you get one for me?" I asked. "If I paid you?"

Gammi visibly withdrew at the prospect. "You don't have enough. Not even your tongue-poppers would persuade me."

Her reaction sent a surge of fear through me. She didn't seem the sort to frighten easily and if she was afraid of Gizler, then I could only conclude I wasn't going to have much fun paying him a visit.

"Whatever you're planning, it's not worth it," she said, with as much sincerity as I'd ever heard her use. "You'd make a nice addition to his store. Loves a new trophy, Gizler does. You'd provide him with endless possibilities."

The prospect of being Gizler's plaything was far from appealing, but if I was to fashion material for Locryn, I had no choice.

"Where can I find his store?" I asked, hoping Gammi didn't notice the tremor in my voice.

She sighed in resignation. "Take the east road, across the hills. He lives in the swamp town near the marshes. You can't miss it."

"Thank you," I said. "Any other tips for when I meet him?" I pulled out a candy. "I'm happy to pay for information."

"Only speak to him in questions. He has an enchantment that binds anyone who makes a statement to him, and he will own you forever. And be prepared to pay a high price for what you seek. These won't be nearly enough there," she said, snatching the sherbet from my hand.

"Thank you," I said. "I appreciate your help."

"Not sure what difference it will make," she said. "Goodbye, girl, it was a pleasure doing business with you."

The realization that Gammi never expected to see me again was far from reassuring, she hadn't acted this way when she sent me into Beattie's lair, but I managed to give her a farewell smile before I left the night market. I knew if I didn't go immediately, I'd talk myself out of what had to be done, and so I walked down the road and away from the court. Whatever price Gizler asked, I'd have to try to pay. And hope I made it back with a spinning wheel and loom.

Or else end up an item on Gizler's shelf.

I hadn't even left the market before someone called my name, and I looked back to see Conor running toward me.

"What are you doing here?" I asked in surprise. "Shouldn't you be asleep?"

"Going through a patch of insomina," he said, and I smiled as he slightly mispronounced the word I'd taught him. "I was walking through the market so I wasn't alone with my thoughts and then who should I see wandering past, looking determined, but my friend who's so obviously been avoiding me."

My blush betrayed my guilt. "I'm sorry," I said. "I've been avoiding everyone."

"It's all right," he said, reaching to touch my shoulder. "This place drives you slowly mad and sometimes you have to do what you can to survive." His fingers squeezed gently, assuring me he understood something of what I was going through, if not the details. "Now," he said, changing the subject. "Are you going anywhere nice?"

I laughed flatly. "I wish. I'm off to pay Gizler the goblin a visit."

"What?" All humor dissolved.

"Shh," I hissed. "Look, I can do it. I'll walk to his delightful-sounding swamp town, pop to his shop, and get what I need. I'll be in and out."

"Have you lost your senses?" Conor was irate. "Did you not hear me when I told you he was the one setting traps in the forest? He's evil, Nettle. You don't 'pop to his shop' and leave with whatever you fancy."

"I'm not stupid," I snapped. "Do you think I actually *want* to go there? Of course I don't! But I need a spinning wheel and a loom and he's the only one round here who sells them apparently. Gammi told me a few things, to give me a chance. Like only speak to him in questions, that sort of thing."

Conor regarded me for a long time, searching my face for some sort of reassurance that I knew what I was doing.

"I'm sorry," I said. "I can't give up, I just can't. I know I should, but—"

"You can't." Conor smiled sadly. "I get it. But you're not going there—"

"I'm not asking for your permission," I shouted, but he took my hand in his.

"I was saying, you're not going there alone."

I stared at him in surprise and shook my head. "No, it's not safe."

Conor groaned. "Stop being so stubborn and let's get this over with."

And with my hand firmly in his, he led the way.

## TWENTY-ONE

I was glad of his company as we followed the road east.

It was an unfamiliar path, to me anyway. Conor seemed to know exactly where we were going.

"At least this thread works," I said with a laugh, pointing to the gold band on my wrist. "I sense this is a long road."

Conor glanced at me. "What do you mean? Does your other one not?"

"Nope. The paths shift all the time. Not just in the forest, but at the palace, in the town. I told Gammi but she insisted there was nothing wrong with the thread."

He looked worried. "I've never heard of the thread failing before." When I met his gaze, I saw something beyond concern. Doubt. "Does it worry you that nothing here affects you quite the same way it does other humans?"

"That's not true, is it?" It came out more defensively than I'd intended.

"Well, there's the thread, the fact that Beattie didn't kill you on sight, you were able to ride Pym, and you need to eat and sleep a lot less than the rest of us."

That was all true, plus there were things I hadn't told him about. The way I could see through glamours sometimes, the way the nettles seemed to speak to me through dreams, or how I could remember about Ketter despite Lassila's best attempts to stop me.

"I've always been a bit strange," I said, searching for an explanation.

He cast me a dubious look.

"I know," I agreed. "You're right, it doesn't make sense. But I don't know what to tell you. I have no more idea than you. Maybe it's because my grandma raised me on faery stories?"

"Maybe." He didn't sound convinced. Worse, he sounded hurt. He knew I was keeping things from him, and as I had pointed out so angrily to Lassila, lying to someone you cared about wasn't love.

"I have to tell you something," I said, knowing it might not end well, but understanding that keeping this information from him wasn't protecting him, but deceiving him. "It won't be easy to hear."

Conor kept walking and gave me space to confess. I told him everything Ellion had said about his task, how he'd failed long ago and any other attempt was pointless. How, ultimately, he was never going home.

He was silent for a while when I stopped talking. Eventually, he shrugged. "At least I know why you've been avoiding me," he said, trying to joke about it.

"Conor—"

"No matter," he interrupted. "There never was much chance I'd make it back, was there? Now I won't waste any more time filling barrows with straw."

"I'm sorry," I said, hating how hollow my words sounded.

"Don't be," he said. "I'm glad you told me. Locryn must have found it satisfying somehow, watching me struggle pointlessly."

"I don't think he even cares enough for that."

"No. No, I don't suppose he does."

We both fell silent, until Conor pointed ahead. "No moping, we need our wits about us. That's where Gizler lives. Are you sure you want to go?"

"We've come all this way. No turning back now," I said, mustering courage I didn't really feel. "Not without my wheel and loom."

But as we followed the road down toward the marshlands and into the grim town, I knew we'd made a mistake. This wasn't anything like Locryn's moorland court. The wet earth was thick like tar, sticking horribly to my bare feet. The smell that permeated the air was repulsive, like putrefying plants and burned wood mingled with melting flesh. In front of us were three wooden buildings, each perched in a tangle of giant vines. One had bubbling cauldrons in its window, another a display of skinned carcasses. I ignored them both, my attention solely on the third. Above its door, which was a patchwork of bones, hung a sign that read 'Gizler.' The goblin had nothing in his window to tempt in passing trade, which could only be a bad thing.

"You don't have to do this," Conor said. "We can go back right now, and you can find some other way to spin your thread."

How I wished I could. "There is no other way." I forced my legs to carry me toward Gizler's store, even though every instinct told me to run the other way.

"You should wait out here," I said to Conor when we reached the door.

"Why? No, I'm coming in."

"We don't want to do anything to provoke him," I said. "I need to earn his trust, and I think two of us will seem more threatening."

I could tell Conor wanted to argue, but he knew I was right. Eventually, he nodded. "I'll be waiting here. And hoping no one else passes by. Not sure I want to meet the kind of people who shop here. This is the worst town I've ever seen."

Though I knew he wasn't entirely joking, I was glad of his humor. "I'll be as quick as I can."

"Remember, only speak in questions."

"Like this?" I grinned.

"Good luck." Conor held up two sets of crossed fingers and I did the same. I needed all the luck I could get.

A dainty bell rang over the door as I pushed it open, a far more delicate sound than I'd been expecting. But I soon realized it was the only pleasant thing in the shop.

The shelves to my right were stacked with jars filled with a murky liquid, in which floating eyeballs turned to observe my arrival. To my left was an array of stuffed animals — not recognizable creatures but made of many random parts. A grotesque specimen appeared to have the back legs of a hare stitched to the body of a badger and a single fox leg at the front. Its head was a crow's and I wondered then whether that was the purpose of Gizler's traps. To collect bodies to dismantle and reassemble in his own vile fashion.

"You like my artwork?"

I started at the voice and saw an ancient man emerging from the back room to stand behind the counter. His long chin jutted, a small tuft of white hair at the end of it, his incredibly bushy eyebrows dominated the top half of his face. He was slight and short too. If I had passed him in the street, I wouldn't have thought him threatening in the least. But I knew enough of this place not to trust appearances.

"Would you like me to admire it?"

My response visibly disappointed him. He had hoped I would fall at the first hurdle and answer without a question. "Is that why you're here?"

"Are you open for business?"

"Do I look closed?"

So he was playing the same game, was he? This was going to be a challenge. He was sure to be more practiced at speaking in questions than I was. My eyes strayed to the wall behind him, covered in clocks. There were a lot more than twelve hours marked on them, which made sense given how unusual time was here. Certainly none of them told the same time, and I gagged when I realized the hands pointing to the hours were actual hands. Some were distinctly human.

Wanting to leave as quickly as possible, I cleared my throat. "Do you have a spinning wheel and a loom I could purchase?"

Gizler wiggled his chin in contemplation. "What do you want them for?"

"What would you expect I would use them for?"

"Have you enough to purchase them?"

Was this his plan? Keep me talking until I tripped up? To be fair, it would probably work. Sooner or later, I would say the wrong thing and forget to form a question. I would have to be careful. "What is your price?"

Gizler scratched his head in thought. "Would you give me that secret you carry?"

I was so tired of being asked that question, but perhaps in this place where questions were so important, I might receive an answer. "What secret?"

"You don't know?" He cackled, a high-pitched laugh. "What worth does it have to me if you are clueless?"

"Then why mention it?" I prickled at his scorn, not in the mood to be taunted by a goblin who delighted in dismembering and reconstructing animals.

My irritation seemed to delight him, and he leaned across the counter, his face too close to mine. "What if I took your teeth, eh? Would you like to see a necklace made from them? Do you think your eyes, along with everything they've ever seen, would make a prettier piece? Or tell me, shall I take your tongue, with every word ever spoken and yet to say? Are you willing to pay any of those?"

I swallowed, fear threatening to drown me. I had been far too confident thinking I could waltz in here and buy what I wanted, that I could outwit such a terrifying adversary. He saw my doubt, my terror, and licked his lips.

"Or shall I take your head for my wall?" he hissed. "You'd be a lovely addition to my collection, don't you think?"

He gestured for me to turn, and I recoiled at the sight. Above the window were mounted heads—animals, hobgoblins, faeries, and at least one human. But they weren't dead. Their mouths were sewn shut so that they couldn't cry out, but their eyes were open, some wide with desperation, while several wept tears of blood.

It was so utterly grotesque, the suffering they were forced to endure so horrific, that it eclipsed my own predicament and raw fury bubbled inside me.

When I turned to face Gizler once more, the whole shop seemed to have fallen into shadow. Uncertainty flickered in his eyes at the change in me and he moved an inch away.

"Do you know who I am?" I asked, not really sure where my running mouth was going to take me but trusting my anger. "Who I work for?"

The room grew darker and Gizler trembled. "I'm sorry," he stuttered. "How could I have known who you were?"

"The King of the Moorland Court demands I complete my work and so I will have what I require, or would you like to explain to him why you have denied me?"

"You will accept Gizler's apology, yes?" Gizler was the one afraid now, and I was truly surprised. I hadn't expected the king's name to carry so much weight with the goblin trader. But I wasn't going to waste the shift in power.

"Will you accept my offer?" I thrust my hand into my pocket, searching for what I had in mind. It wasn't easy to free it, but seconds later, I held a needle aloft, like a teeny tiny sword. Inwardly, I groaned. I had hoped to grab my spare needle, but instead I was holding out my favorite. Oh well, I couldn't do anything about that now. "In exchange for a spinning wheel and loom, will you take this mighty needle as payment?"

Gizler stared at it in wonder. "What is it? I smell iron, but what else is it?"

"Have you never heard of the legendary stainless steel?" Honestly, I had no idea whether that's what the needle was made from, it could be nickel-plated, or who knew what, but Gizler didn't know and so I was going to run with it and make it sound priceless. "Do you not know that it is the most powerful of all the metals in the human world? And the only one of its kind in all the faery realm?"

"Yes, yes, will you give it to Gizler?" He beckoned urgently with his fingers for me to pass it over.

"Will you show me the wheel and loom first? Can I satisfy myself that I am not overpaying?"

With a flick of his wrist, the two items appeared to my left, and I smiled to myself. They were perfect.

"How will I take them home?"

"I can send them, if you wish?"

"You can do that?"

Gizler nodded and with a wave, the items disappeared. "They're in your barn, so will you hand over the needle now?"

"I will, but will you also set those poor people free from their torment?" I gestured to the pitiful heads.

Gizler's eyes narrowed. I was pushing my luck, but I had to try, I couldn't leave them there to suffer. I wiggled the needle tantalizingly.

"Yes, yes, do we have a deal?"

I so nearly failed at the last moment, was so close to uttering the word "deal" and binding my soul to his, but caught myself just in time. "Are my wheel and loom waiting in my barn?"

"I said so, didn't I?"

He practically snatched the needle from my hand, as I turned and forced myself to walk calmly out of his shop.

Conor leaped from where he waited and rushed to me.

"What the hell happened in there? Where did that shadow come from?"

I glanced back at the shop and realized the whole building was cloaked in darkness. No wonder Gizler had been afraid.

"Not here," I said, grabbing Conor's arm. "Let's leave before he changes his mind."

As we ran fast back along the road toward the relative safety of Locryn's court, I knew I'd only survived for one reason. A shadow faery whose king really wanted me to succeed with this task. And though the last thing I wanted was to be indebted to him, I probably owed Ellion my life.

# TWENTY-TWO

The spinning wheel and loom were exactly where Gizler had said they would be. He might be evil, but at least he was honest in his deal-making.

The fact that my knowledge of how to spin or weave was limited to watching Grandma when I was younger seemed somehow unimportant in the scheme of things. Besides, I still had some retted stalks to pry open and fibers to separate, as well as needing to prepare them as the dream girl had before she began to spin.

I worked relentlessly, forcing myself to take an occasional break to visit Conor. We didn't speak of his task again, but he seemed to have found a kind of peace about his situation. Our conversations fell back into the easy kind they had been before, where he asked me questions about home and I told him all I could remember. This was his only connection to the human realm now and he was clinging to it fast.

Under the waning moons, as I sat combing through the fibers with the bone knife Ellion had first given me to cut the nettles, the shadow faery appeared.

I hadn't seen him since the ball, when I'd discovered the dream-walkers and he'd brought me safely away. I tried not to think about how he'd unlaced my gown, and failed, blushing almost immediately.

"What can I do for you?" I asked, trying to pretend I wasn't pleased to see him.

"I'm here on the king's business," he said without preamble, and my spirits sank. He hadn't come because he missed me then.

"Oh, what does the king want now?"

"He wishes to dine with you."

Nerves made me laugh. "He hates me. Why would he want to spend any time with me?"

"I believe he wishes to speak about your progress." Ellion's jaw had never been so clenched.

"So tell him. You report back on everything else."

He ignored my scathing remark, instead stepping toward me, and that was when I realized how worried he was.

"Nettle, you need to be careful," he said. "The king has grown morose and ever more unpredictable. He hasn't attended a ball for many nights, not even briefly. He barely leaves his chamber and obsesses over the mirror."

"Ah. He wants to know how close I am to allowing him to break the enchantment she placed on him."

Ellion inclined his head. He hadn't realized I knew what the king intended.

"The less you know, the better," he replied.

"For me? Or for you?"

Ellion sighed. "Must you argue with me on every matter? You are the most vexing and frustrating person I ever met."

His lips, the angle of his jaw, the contours of his cheekbones, intoxicated me. I wanted to stay there and drink him in, every line of him, and even if it was some enchantment making him so beautiful, I didn't care. He was the sun at the center of the shadows, and I longed to bask in his warmth.

I stepped away from him, terrified of the feelings he stirred in me. "I should thank you for your help at Gizler's. Pretty sure my head would be mounted on his wall by now if it weren't for you."

"You went to Gizler's?"

I rolled my eyes. "You don't have to pretend. I know you keep an eye on me and do what you have to so that this task is completed."

"Nettle . . ." Ellion moved toward me, but I raised my hand, forcing him to keep his distance.

"I keep having dreams," I said, the words tumbling from me, as I desperately needed to tell someone, knowing Ellion wouldn't judge me. "Every time I sleep since I came here with the nettles. I dream of someone who looks like me. I thought it was me at first, but I was wrong, we're just similar. She's the one showing me how to turn the nettles to cloth."

"Who is she?"

I shook my head. "I don't know. I think she needs my help though. She doesn't talk to me, but I have a feeling that something bad is happening to her. Or is going to. She's pregnant."

Ellion frowned as he considered this, but he only said, "We have to go. The king is waiting, and you need to be prepared."

"Prepared?"

He pulled me to his chest and transported me to a room within the palace, where several faeries were standing ready.

"Be quick," Ellion commanded. "Locryn grows impatient."

I was shuffled behind a screen, where my dress was swiftly removed. Many hands piled my hair on my head, pinning it in place with gems like perfect drops of blood. A gown of deep crimson was given to me to step into, and I sensed immediately this was Beattie's work. I shuddered to think how much actual blood had been spilled to create such a rich color. The bodice was encrusted with black crystals, sparkling like chips of onyx. It pinched in at the waist, before flowing into a full skirt, thick with netting and a trailing pattern of black thread as if a shadow spider had spun her finest silk across the material. The two black wings at my back were made from the same material, as was the veil that was placed to hide my face.

"Is she ready?" Ellion urged, and seconds later I was shoved out to face him.

I did a twirl. "Will I do?"

"The king will be pleased," he said, and gestured for me to follow him.

"You don't like the dress?" I asked, as we walked through a stony corridor.

He stared straight ahead. "I like you when your hair is wild and your feet are bare. When there are straw and twigs caught in your dress, when dirt is smeared on your cheek and when I can see your hazel eyes and watch how the green dances within them. This dress is good enough. But you are most beautiful when you are just as you are."

Tears filled my eyes. I wasn't sure I had ever felt so seen. So accepted. He'd stunned me completely. I hadn't even noticed that we'd reached a door, and I tried to recover my breath when he knocked on it.

"Ellion," I began, but the door opened and he indicated I should go through.

I was in Locryn's private chambers, just as they had been when I'd hidden behind one of the granite standing stones and spied on him. The only difference was the embroidered cloth covering what I knew was Keita's mirror.

Locryn stood before a table piled high with food and was wearing the most lavish outfit I'd ever seen. Two capped sleeves made from iridescent beetle shells were attached to strings of pearl-like water droplets that acted as braces, joining shimmering pants that changed color like a starling's wing in the sunlight. He looked incredibly handsome.

"Human, welcome," he said, waving Ellion away.

I snatched a last look at Ellion before he left me alone with the king.

"Your Majesty," I said, unnerved by Locryn's sudden charm. "Thank you for this honor."

"Come, eat."

I couldn't help but glance at the mirror as I took my seat opposite him, noting that he positioned himself so that he could see it at all times.

There were honeyed fruits and sweet pastries, and I thought of Grandma. What would she say if she could see me sitting with the faery king and sharing his food?

*Nothing good*, I mused to myself with a chuckle.

"I'll confess I'm surprised to be here," I said, as I took a fondant cake that shimmered like oil in water. I left it on the side of my plate. "After our previous encounters."

"Yes, you are the first human ever to be permitted in my quarters. I hear they call you Nettle."

"They do," I agreed, wondering whether Ellion had framed it that way on purpose. He hadn't directly given Locryn my name, but rather had made it sound like a nickname because of my affinity with the plant.

"You have had rather more success than most with

your tasks," he observed, popping a silver mushroom into his mouth.

How many deals had he made over the centuries he'd ruled? How many humans had he deceived and destroyed? And he dared sit there and say that to me?

I couldn't think of a reply that didn't sound snarky, so I smiled.

"You've enjoyed your time at my court?" he asked, as though we were old friends catching up. "I hear you've attended the masquerade balls."

"I think we can assume Ellion has reported my every movement to you," I said, causing Locryn to laugh.

"You cannot blame me for wanting to keep an eye on you. You've intrigued me. Something no human has ever managed before."

"Because you believe I may be able to deliver something you want." This time I couldn't disguise the coldness in my voice. Locryn's eyes narrowed.

"And what might that be, do you imagine?"

"Your Majesty, let us stop this game. From the moment you heard that I fell through a portal of nettles, the seed of an idea has been growing in your mind, has it not? Of a way to harness their protective magic? And now you sense that such a goal may be within your reach, is that right? If you want to know how long you have to wait, you can ask. You're the king. You don't need to pretend with all this." I gestured to the food and my gown.

Locryn's face twitched with repressed anger. Inside I felt I might faint away at my boldness, but I held my ground.

"Can it be done?" he surprised me by asking. Such a response showed me how desperately he wanted it.

I thought of Beattie's warnings, of Ellion's and Conor's. Do not trust the king was the message shouted loud and clear. But I pressed on regardless.

"I think so," I said. "The question is, should it?"

Locryn frowned. "What do you mean?"

Reaching for an unfamiliar berry, I placed it next to the cake and left it untouched. The king tried to maintain his composure, but his rage was bubbling beneath the surface. I had something he wanted, and I was going to take a chance.

"If the magic of the nettles can be harnessed, what would you use it for? Good or ill?"

His fury erupted. "You dare question your king?"

"You are not my king," I reminded him. "And yes, I do, because I don't understand why you would need protective magic."

We stared at each other a while longer, until Locryn leaned back, wiping his fingers clean on a napkin.

"Have you ever been in love, human?" Even knowing my name, he couldn't bring himself to use it.

"So this is about your queen," I said.

"Everything is about her," he said, the words sounding simultaneously loving and sinister. After a brief consideration, he stood. "I want to show you something," he said, and strode to the mirror.

In a single sweep, he pulled the cloth from it, revealing a window into the forest court.

Keita was sitting on a throne of winter roses tangled with thorns. The tiny leaves in her hair were covered in frost, her skin tinged with blue, her lips covered in small ice crystals. Her handmaidens tended to her, brushing her hair, feeding her sugared treats, reading her a story. The happiness that radiated from them was evident.

"She is beautiful, is she not?" he asked, though I knew he wasn't expecting an answer. "Never in my life have I met her equal." He reached his hand to the glass to caress her face. "Once it was me who made her happy."

Then he turned to me, and his eyes shone. "To begin with, I believed this was her way to punish me for our argument, that I would be forced to see that she didn't need me anymore. But it has been too long." He glanced back at the mirror. "Too long," he echoed to her. When he faced me again, it was with resolve. "I believe this is a trick, an illusion. The magic she first cast has persisted and now conceals the truth, as recently I have seen her in my dreams. She calls to me, begs for my help, weeps for my return. Something is wrong, and I have to reach her, have to rescue her."

He rendered me speechless, it was so far from what I was expecting him to say. "You think this isn't real?"

I asked, looking at Keita's dazzling smile and finding it hard to believe it wasn't genuine.

"How can she be that happy without me?" he shouted, causing me to flinch. "For a time, perhaps, yes. I too lost myself to endless pleasures when we first separated. But now I cannot find joy in dancing or eating or hunting and so, no! I do not believe this is real."

He stepped toward me, closer than he'd ever come before and stared at me intensely. "Your nettles don't just possess protective magic. They have the power to *repel* magic. That's why I need them. With your garment I believe I will at last be able to circumvent the barrier she has placed between us, and then I shall save her from the danger she is in."

Ellion was right. Locryn was behaving erratically. "What if you go there and find she actually is happy?" I whispered.

"Then I shall at least have a chance to bid her farewell," he said. "But I cannot take the risk. Cannot abandon her while she calls to me in need." He searched my face, though the veil must have obscured it. "Wouldn't you do anything to return to the one you love?"

And there it was. He might be a jealous and unreasonable husband, furious to have been spurned by his wife who had made it abundantly clear she didn't need him, but who was I to question him? Beattie had asked me whether I should give him what he wanted. But it wasn't just about him. This was about what I wanted.

I made my choice. "Everything I'm doing here is so that I can go home to my grandmother. So yes, I would do anything."

Locryn's eyes shone with triumph. "Then you should get back to work."

# Twenty-Three

I refused Locryn's offer for Ellion to escort me back to my barn and chose instead to clear my head in the fresh night air. I wasn't sure Ellion would approve of the decision I had just made, although he possibly already knew, if he had been watching from the shadows.

Dawn wasn't far away, but the scarlet stars still scattered the violet sky with sharp brilliance. It was truly beautiful in a place where so much beauty was an illusion, conjured to deceive. How ironic that the king hated the thought he was on the receiving end of trickery when he himself was the master of it.

I found myself at the yard and a calm settled over me. I hadn't been here since Morcan had forbidden me to come near the horses, but I knew he wouldn't be around now. There was a lot of comfort to be drawn from this place.

The squeak of a barrow made me glance up and there, at the far end of the yard, was Conor.

Our eyes met and he smiled.

"Goodness," he said, resting the barrow and walking toward me. "You look wonderful."

"Thanks, it's one of Beattie's creations, so it's probably soaked in enchantments." But I blushed nonetheless.

"I didn't know there was a masquerade tonight," he said.

"There wasn't. I've just had dinner with the king."

Conor's brow furrowed. "I think I must be imagining things, because it sounded like you just said you had dined with Locryn, that well-known hater of humans."

I laughed. "I can assure you no one was more surprised than me."

"What did he want?"

"Oh, to check up on how the garment was coming along. He thinks the queen is in danger and is desperate to reach her, using the magic in the nettles to break her enchantment."

Conor pulled a face. "Do you believe him?"

"I think when it comes to Keita, he cannot be objective. He is in love."

It was only then it occurred to me that Conor shouldn't be here in the yard either. He should be sleeping. I was about to ask him what he was doing, but then I realized, and sadness overwhelmed me.

"You're still trying to do your task."

He managed a shy smile. "I know what you said, but what if Ellion was tricking you? What if it was a lie to make me give up? I can't do that anymore than you can. I want to go home." His voice caught and he blinked away unwanted tears. "So tell me, does the king live in luxury? I imagine his chambers are better than a hayloft."

"Everything about the palace is breathtaking," I said. "His rooms, the food, the music, the dresses." I gestured to my gown. "All exquisite." I sighed. "But it's not real. Nothing here is, everything is a lie."

"I'm real," Conor said, holding out his hand. "Dance with me?"

"What, here?" I asked.

"Why not? I may not be dressed for the occasion, but you are and the rest we can pretend."

"I'm tired of pretending," I said, taking his hand, and letting him pull me close.

He smelled of horse and straw, and it was more wonderful than any of the faery perfumes. I rested my head against his shoulder and breathed deeply, as we moved in time to silent music.

"I could do this every night," Conor murmured into my hair.

"Me too," I said, realizing how much I relied on his steadiness. In this unpredictable and confusing world, he was the constant that anchored me. Being with him was easy.

We laughed and danced beneath the scarlet stars, and in the sanctuary of each other's arms nothing else mattered.

Slowly, the sun began to rise, the stars fading to pinpricks on a rosy-pink sky, and reality shattered the dream.

"I should go," I said. "Or I'll never finish my task."

"You will," he breathed, holding me tightly. "You'll succeed."

I wanted to believe him, but I couldn't. I wanted to tell him everything. The secrets I had tucked away, the fears I carried. It was too late though.

I stole one last moment in his arms before bidding him farewell and returning to my barn.

After that, I lived and breathed working on my namesake nettles. It turned out, that despite not having spun before, I had a natural instinct for it. More than that, I loved it. There was something calming about whiling away the sunlight at the spinning wheel, turning the fibers into thread, entranced at the process.

Never had I felt closer to my grandma than while I was spinning, all the hours I'd spent as a child watching her were paying off. Not only had I absorbed her technique, but I associated the clack of the pedal, the sigh of the wheel with happy evenings spent with her.

# Nettle

Sometimes Conor brought me food and asked how I was progressing, but he didn't ever stay long, sensing I wasn't to be disturbed from the task in hand. Other times I was aware of Ellion watching from the shadows, though he never spoke to me, nor I to him. But his silent companionship comforted me.

Occasionally, I wondered if perhaps the spinning wheel was enchanted, some magic of Gizler's on it to cast a trance over whoever used it. I didn't care, I could have stayed there forever, watching the wheel turn like time itself, but soon there were no more nettle fibers to spin, and I was ready to begin weaving on the loom.

Like the spinning, my knowledge was limited to what I'd seen my grandma do. I knew enough to clumsily set up the loom with vertical warp threads and to use the wooden shuttle to weave the weft threads in and out horizontally, using a beater to force everything down tightly. I wasn't going to win any prizes for perfection, but I knew that didn't matter. All Locryn cared about was whether this cloth would allow him to harness the nettles' potent magic.

As the fabric grew, my thoughts drifted to what I would make from it, and how I might embellish it. It seemed only right to use the dried nettle leaves I'd discarded, but I would need thread to stitch them on.

So as the silver moon rose, I took a break from weaving to visit Gammi for what I hoped would be the last time. As I only had a single lemon sherbet left, any future visits could cost me more than I was willing to pay.

"You're alive!" she gasped as I approached. "Did you think better of visiting Gizler then?"

"No, I went, and I survived, thanks to you. Without your advice, I would have certainly been a head on his wall by now."

Gammi bowed. "Here to help my favorite customers. Now, what can I do for you tonight?"

"I'm looking for some thread to stitch with, something beautiful but steeped in magic. Good magic, something that will enhance the power already bound in the cloth."

I had no idea whether such a thing existed, but Gammi scratched her chin and searched about her table. She pulled out a tangled ball of starlike thread and pressed it into my hand.

"That will do the trick," she said. "That's a Gammi guarantee."

"Thank you," I said, retrieving the sticky candy from my pocket. I hesitated. Once this was gone, that was it, no more food from home. I had to remind myself that I would have so much more when I completed my deal. Still, as I handed it over, a sense of loss passed through me, as though I had just seen the last of something precious.

It was a relief to return to my barn, where the rhythm and pattern of the weaving calmed me like a mysterious lullaby.

Light brightened and dimmed within these walls as sun and moons took many turns and eventually, the cloth was finished.

It was coarse and far from perfect, but if I'd possessed a single remaining shred of energy, I would have marveled at my achievement. However, I wasn't done yet. Now I had to turn it into a garment for the king.

I already knew I couldn't compete with Beattie, so I wasn't going to try. It had to be simple, because my skills were limited. There really was only one garment that seemed right.

I would make a cloak.

My penknife sufficed to cut the cloth into shape, and I tucked the offcuts safely away. After the endless hours of love and labor I'd spent on it, I wasn't prepared to waste a scrap.

I dug out my old sewing kit, annoyed to have given Gizler my favorite needle. The slightly rusty needle would have to do. I used some of the thread from home to start with, stitching a hem until my fingers bled and my eyes ached.

When that task was complete, it was time to add the embellishments. I used Gammi's thread to attach both dried nettle leaves and the pressed white nettle flowers, feeling the magic flowing into the cloak with every stitch, enhancing the finish to a level far beyond my own capabilities.

The night before I finished, I dreamed again.

I slept little these days and when I did, I dreamed only of mist. I could not find the pregnant girl, or the loom I'd seen her working at.

Tonight I was determined to solve the mystery.

I ran through the haze calling to her and was beginning to give up hope, when I heard the sound of sobbing. Running toward it, the cloud swirled about me thicker and faster, until it suddenly lifted and there she was.

She was kneeling on the forest floor, clutching a bundle to her chest as she wept.

Cautiously, I approached, wanting to comfort her, sensing nothing could. Her sobs turned to wails and she curled in a ball, crying as if her world had ended.

I moved closer and stared at the bundle, which she'd dropped beside her. The material was all too familiar, I had spent enough time creating my own. Nettle cloth woven into a small blanket, perfect for a baby.

And I knew then why she cried. Her world *had* ended. Her child was gone. The blanket was all she had left. Nothing that could be said or done would change that.

I woke with tears streaming down my face. The girl's pain had been raw and real, as if her grief was my own.

Doing the only thing I could, I picked up the cloak to add the final touches, using what remained of Gammi's thread to embroider the outline of nettle leaves around the neckline.

At last, the thread ran out and there was nothing left to do but stare in disbelief at what I'd created. I felt no elation, no pride now. Only sadness that I couldn't shake.

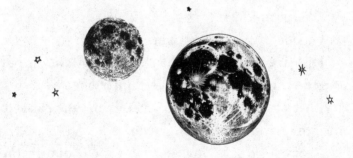

# Twenty-Four

"Ellion," I whispered into the air, knowing he would hear me. "I need to see the king."

He appeared from the shadows and immediately his eyes fixed on the cloak in my hands.

"You've finished."

I nodded. "Will you take me to him?"

His gaze moved from the cloth to my face. As our eyes met, I saw my own uncertainty reflected in his. Neither of us was convinced that giving the cloak to the king was the right thing to do.

"Come," he said, inviting me to join him in the darkness, where he transported me to the corridor outside Locryn's chamber in a heartbeat.

"Thanks," I said. "I appreciate you saving me the walk." I gave him a weak smile.

"I did nothing," he said, and when I frowned, he added, "Only shadow faeries can move through shadows, Nettle."

"What . . . ?" I began, but before my thoughts could take shape, the door burst open, and Locryn stood before us.

He recoiled at the sight of me without a veil, and Ellion acted quickly to magic one from shadow. With my face hidden, the king recovered himself.

"You have it?" he asked, beckoning us in.

"I do." I held out the folded garment.

Locryn stared at my offering, his hand hovering just above it. "Is it possible?" he murmured. "To touch such a thing?"

He grasped it. When nothing bad happened, he shook it out, revealing it in all its splendor. "A cloak!" he exclaimed. "Made of nettles. And I can hold it." He admired it, before throwing it about his shoulders. "It may be the plainest thing I possess, but this is wonderous. I cannot believe you did it."

Nor could I, but I didn't want him to know that.

"Ellion, try to kill me," Locryn said, swishing about to see how the cloak moved.

I'm not sure who was more shocked, me or Ellion.

"Your Majesty?" Ellion must have thought he'd misheard.

"Come, Ellion, I know you've wanted to more than once over the millennia. Here's your chance. Strike me with your most powerful magic."

When Ellion continued to hesitate, Locryn grew angry.

"I have given you an order," he said, his eyes burning with rage. "Would you defy your king?"

Ellion glared at him. And then he raised both hands, sending a lethal rush of magic at the king.

Nothing happened.

Locryn was jubilant. "It works!" he cried. "It protected me."

"Forgive me, Your Majesty," Ellion said, bowing before his king.

Locryn brushed him away. "You did only as I asked."

"Then, if I may, what do you intend to do now you possess such a garment?"

"Now I rescue my bride," Locryn said, and he uncovered the mirror, gazing longingly at the scene it showed.

Keita was seated at a stone table held up by twisted hazel twigs. She was alone, eating a banquet for one, the table covered with a mouthwatering assortment of pastries. Between bites, she closed her eyes in contentment.

"You see how this image deceives me?" Locryn murmured. "Nobody is that happy when they eat."

I thought of me and Grandma sneaking raspberries from the cane while we picked them for making jam, and begged to differ.

Ellion didn't seem convinced either. "If it is reconciliation you seek, do you think entering into her court uninvited is the best way to go about things?"

"She is my queen!" Locryn roared, and in that flare

of temper, I saw a sliver of his true face beneath the glamour, distorted and cruel. "She banished me! I owe her nothing, in fact, I should punish her for the suffering she has caused me." He took a breath and regained his self-control. "But I am merciful, and even after all she has done, I am willing to save her from the torment I know she is in. There isn't a moment to lose."

"Please consider what you're doing." Ellion tried to reason with his king, though it was pointless. Locryn had been planning this for some time and was not to be dissuaded.

He walked to the mirror and brushed his hand against the frame. Then he turned to look at me.

"You will accompany me," he said.

"No!" I cried and when his eyes blazed, I tried to soften my response. "If it's all the same to you, I would rather not."

Locryn stepped toward me. "You think that because you have crafted such a powerful garment, you can refuse me?"

I met Ellion's worried gaze, before turning my attention back to Locryn. "Do you think taking me is a good idea? If she's in trouble, what use will I be?"

The king fixed me with a terrifying glare. "If you do not come with me, then you will not be given a third task, and your deal will never be completed."

Deceit and trickery. I should have known.

"Why me?" I whispered.

"Because it was Keita who brought you to me. When you explained how you came to be here, I knew at once it had to be her doing. To begin with I assumed it was her fondness for your kind, but then I realized. She needed to be rescued, had to find a way to send word of her pain and so she allowed you through the portal, sensing your affinity to nettles."

Did he truly believe this? Or had years of heartbreak undone him?

"If I go with you, you'll give me my final task?" I wanted him to promise.

Locryn nodded. "I will. Now come, let us visit my queen."

Before I could even bid Ellion goodbye, Locryn stepped into the mirror, the cloak permitting him to pass through and drag me behind him.

We were immediately transported to the glade, before the table, the trees surrounding it covered in feathers instead of leaves, soft and dreamy. It was exactly as it had appeared in the mirror, apart from the content expression on Keita's face rapidly giving way to horror.

"*You?*" she hissed, rising to her feet. "*How . . . ?*"

I looked at Locryn, who was staring at Keita in disbelief. "It's really you," he gasped.

"Of course it's me," she snapped, and I was in awe of her glorious anger. If she had appeared beautiful in the mirror, that did not compare to standing in her presence. Her power filled the air, which hummed with peril.

I had never seen Locryn like this. He dwindled in her brilliance, and I realized the mirror had never lied. Keita had been happy without him. It was he who was nothing without her.

"I cast a spell so that you could never come here," she said. "Because I never, ever wanted to see you again. Now leave, before I call my guards."

"No," he said, with a shake of his head. "I came to rescue you."

She laughed. "From what? My perfectly wonderful existence?"

He faltered, before trying again. "Keita, there is much to say."

She gazed at him with contempt. "You can start by telling me how you broke my barrier spell."

Locryn lifted his cloak. "With this. Fashioned from nettles."

Keita dismissed him. "You lie. That is not possible."

"Actually it is," I said, unaware my input was not welcome.

The queen scrutinised me coldly. "Who is this?"

"The girl you brought through a portal of nettles."

Keita looked bored. "I brought no one. Now leave."

That caught Locryn off guard, and a glimmer of uncertainty passed over his face, but then to my surprise—and Keita's—he threw himself at her feet.

"I implore you, forgive me, my queen. I have suffered endlessly without you. I cannot bear the emptiness your absence has left in my heart. Please, you are the reason I breathe, do not send me away again."

It was embarrassing, and I couldn't begin to understand why I'd been brought along to witness it. For her part, Keita seemed amused.

"Well, well," she said. "You always were pathetic, Locryn. Get up, you're a king, not a worm." When he staggered back to his feet, Keita observed him coolly. "Tell me, are you ready to apologize for what you did?"

"Yes," he replied. "I am changed. I brought a gift to show you."

I wondered what this present might be, before realizing they were both looking at me.

"Her?" Keita scoffed. "What would I want with her?"

"You always wished to own a human and I never permitted it," he said. "But I give her to you now, to prove my devotion, to show I've changed. That I will give you anything you want if only we can be together again."

"I am not yours to give away!" I cried. "What about our deal? What about my third task?"

Locryn's expression turned my blood to ice. "I'm renegotiating the terms."

"No! I don't agree, you can't do that. I have to go home!"

"I'm not sure an insolent human is quite the wonderful gift you think it is," Keita said, turning to study me more closely. "I am perfectly able to find my own human pet."

"You think I would bring you any ordinary human? No, this one possesses a special quality. It is she who made this cloak," Locryn said. "She is a rare thing—a useful human, who would be a valuable addition to your court. Consider what she has achieved for me and then ask what she might do for you?"

That intrigued the queen. "Is it true? You made this garment that allowed my estranged husband to trespass into my lands?"

I sensed the trap, but I only had the truth left. "Yes."

"Then you should be punished," she snarled, and she snatched my veil away.

She stared at me, paling in shock. The atmosphere shifted, I could tell Locryn sensed it too, and I had no idea what was going on. And then Keita uttered the last word I was expecting.

"Nettle?"

# Twenty-Five

"Nettle?" the queen repeated, frowning as her eyes roamed over my face. "No, you aren't her. But you look so like her."

"How do you know my name?" I asked, sensing it might be the most important question I'd ever asked.

Her cunning features sharpened. "*Your* name?" She stepped backwards, her hand pressed to her heart. "No, this is too cruel, Locryn, even for you."

I had no idea what she was talking about and judging from the expression on her husband's face, neither did he.

"I don't know what you mean," he said. "She is nothing more than a gift."

"You come here demanding forgiveness and then remind me of why I banished you in the first place? Why?"

With Locryn lost for words, I seized my opportunity.

"What did he do? To hurt you so deeply? Because no one in his realm knows."

She gave a humorless laugh. "Yes, I'm sure he wouldn't want anyone to know the depravity he is capable of, the pain he would willingly inflict."

"Tell me," I said, needing to know.

"He stole the most precious thing in the world from me," the queen said, looking past me to meet Locryn's gaze. A single tear spilled from her eye. "He stole my child."

The truth hung in the air, and I released a long breath. "You had a child?"

"Yes, the most beautiful faery child," Keita said in a rush of emotion. "She was my world and he took her from me. Now can you understand why I banished him? How I can never forgive him for what he did."

My heart clenched. "Why would bringing me here remind you of that?"

She met my gaze and I saw her uncertainty. "I . . ." Her voice trailed off.

I turned to Locryn. A strange calm had come over me, as if the pieces of my life were falling into place. "What did you do with the child you stole?" I asked him, but I knew the answer before it left his lips.

"I took her to the human world, to die there as a changeling."

A tear trickled down my cheek. There was the truth. My truth. Or some of it at least.

"The woman I reminded you of named Nettle," I said to Keita. "Who is she?"

"No one," she said, but her lie held no sway with me.

"*Who is she?*" I shouted as shadows formed about us.

"She was my handmaiden. I'm served by plant faeries and she was the nettle faery."

I needed a moment to be able to form words. "It was her child, wasn't it? Not yours."

"You have to understand, faery babies are rare," Keita said. "When Nettle told me she had fallen pregnant, I knew this precious gift must be mine. I am the queen, after all. A treasure such as a faery baby belonged to me. I loved the child, as if she was my own." She stabbed a finger at Locryn. "You took her from me."

"Because you loved her more than me!" he raged.

"I wasn't yours to take!" I screamed and by now I was practically consumed by the shadows I'd summoned. "Either of yours! *You* snatched me from my mother." I pointed at Keita, before turning my wrath on Locryn. "While *you* left me in another world to die."

Ellion had known, he'd been trying to tell me, to make me see. When had he realized? Had he always been aware of a kindred spirit in me? Or was it only after he discovered he could move me through shadows with him? I thought of the time the leaflings led me to his glade, where the trees had permitted me to enter. I think he knew then. I'd been so blind. That was why Gammi's thread hadn't worked for me, why paths shifted at my command, and why Lassila's magic hadn't affected me. It wasn't Ellion who saved me at Gizler's — that was all me, my anger summoning my shadows. Even Beattie had known, she had told me exactly what I was, but I'd simply misunderstood her. Not anymore.

At last I accepted what I was. A changeling who had come back. A shadow faery.

Keita was staring at me with faint affection. "You're alive."

Locryn was still struggling though. "But how? How could you possibly have survived? I didn't switch you with another, didn't leave you in a warm cradle."

"Because a good woman found me and raised me as her own," I said, my voice breaking with grief. "She kept me near the veil, so I wouldn't fade away. We lived on our own faery hill and she fed me all your stories to keep that part of me alive."

Oh, Grandma. She had feared they would come for me. That's why the mirrors were covered, superstitions observed. She couldn't bear to lose me.

The three of us stood there in a state of shock, not knowing what to do now. It was Locryn who broke the silence, attempting to turn the situation to his advantage.

"I knew from the start that there was something about her," he said to his queen. "See, Keita, I have returned what I stole, paid what I owed."

"You both owe *me*," I said, my voice ice-cold. "You are equally guilty of the crimes committed, you are both the villains in my story. And so I am minded to renegotiate the terms of our deal."

Locryn's eyes narrowed. "What is it you want?"

"A life for a life. You took mine, now you must release another."

I could tell he wasn't happy, but whether because he truly felt some remorse, or he wanted to impress Keita, he nodded.

"You owe my grandma too, because she kept me alive. So you will keep your word and heal her."

Again, he reluctantly agreed.

"And there shall be no third task. Our deal is concluded."

He opened his mouth to object, but a sharp glance from Keita prompted him to accept. I should feel victorious, but I felt nothing.

While I stood trying to process everything that had happened, my shadows dispersing, Keita went to her husband and rested her hand upon his cheek.

"I was so angry with you," she whispered. "I didn't understand how you could take something precious from me."

He gazed at her. "I thought I was losing you and I couldn't bear it. I feared I wouldn't survive without you and when I lost you anyway, I learned how true that was."

"You fool," she said, softly. "I never loved the child more than you. I loved you both equally and differently."

He took her hand in his and pressed it against his lips. "Can you forgive me, my queen?"

Keita reached her free hand to brush a lock of his hair from his face. "As it would seem the child is unharmed and all grown up, I suppose I can." She kissed him, softly at first, then passionately.

It was unbelievable to behold really, the fickleness of the fae. They had been at war for so many years, each angry at the other when they had wronged a mother and child. Yet how easily they claimed their happy ending, while there was none for me.

*Nettle.*

The voice reached me, a tender touch to my aching soul, and now I understood who had been calling to me.

"What happened to your Nettle?" I asked the queen.

"She went to live in the forest," she said dismissively. "I do not recall where."

Something rose inside me, something very like hope.

Leaving the king and queen to their reunion, I went out of the glade and into the forest.

*Nettle.*

The voice was clearer than it had ever been and I followed it as I had in my dream. Only this time I was wide awake. When I reached a wall of mist, my heart started to race as I pushed through, knowing who I would find beyond it.

Among the trees and the many dense patches of nettles stood the girl from my dreams. What I hadn't seen before was how her green dress was made of fresh nettles, or the way the plants seemed to grow from her wrists and trail up her arms. Or her delicate leafy wings.

"Mother?" The word felt strange in my mouth, I'd never used it like this before.

Her hand flew to her mouth as she cried out.

"It was you, wasn't it?" I whispered. "Whose voice I heard all those years. And the silver bells."

She smiled as the tears spilled from her eyes. "I wanted you to know you were never forgotten," she said. "Never alone. And when you asked for help that day, I answered, my nettles bringing you home. I've been trying to keep you safe ever since."

"Thank you." I flung myself into her arms, fitting perfectly into her embrace.

When we let go of each other, I laughed. "The dreams? Did you give me those too?"

She nodded. "I knew we shared the power of the nettles' magic. It was the only way I could communicate with you. I hoped you'd understand my guidance to make the cloth, so that the enchantment would be broken and we might be free to meet again."

"It worked," I breathed. "We did it."

"*You* did it," she said. "The cloth I made wasn't enough."

She reached into a nettle patch and extracted the blanket I had seen in my dreams.

"When I learned I was with child, I confided in my queen. I loved her so much and believed she loved me too. She assured me that she would take care of me. I believed her, but I spent the time before your birth making you this blanket to give you protection. I knew the danger you faced as such a rare thing. But it didn't stop the queen snatching you from your cradle and taking you as her own."

I clutched her hands in mine. "It wasn't your fault."

"Perhaps," she said, tilting her head. "But what matters is that you have found your way home. We have all the time we could wish for to get to know each other."

Time. It wasn't something I had.

I leaned forward and kissed her cheek. "I love you," I said. "I can't stay though. There's something I have to do."

Her lip trembled. "I understand. I'll find you again," she promised. "Listen for my voice on the wind."

And though it tore me apart to leave, I turned and ran.

# TWENTY-SIX

I stood in the forest before the twisted rowan tree trunks, nervous energy making me pace.

"Nettle."

I looked up in relief as Conor approached and held out my hand for him to take.

"What's going on?" he asked. "Ellion told me where to find you. He said I needed to say goodbye."

I nodded, dislodging the tears I was trying to hold back. "That's right," I said. "I renegotiated the terms of my deal. It's time to go home."

Conor's face fell. I could tell he was trying to push his own feelings aside to support me. Because that was the kind of person he was. Decent and kind.

"I'm happy for you," he said, swallowing hard. "You deserve it. But I can't lie. I am going to miss you."

I smiled. "I'm going to miss you too," I said. "I wouldn't have survived here without you, you know that? You taught me how to live, showed me friendship in a way no one else ever has, and I will never, ever forget you." I brushed the tear from his cheek. "Now it's time for you to go home."

He stared at me, puzzled. "What do you mean?"

"The terms of my deal were a life for a life. Your life. You are free to go."

"Nettle, no," he protested. "I can't . . ."

"Yes, you can. These trees will bring you to a forest close to a hill. You're going to go there, find my grandma, and look after her, will you do that? And then you're going to discover all the many incredible ways the world has changed since you were last in it."

I saw hope in his eyes, even as he refused to believe me. "It doesn't make sense. Why would you give up the chance to see her again?"

The truth was I could barely stand the thought, but so many choices had been made for me in my life, and now this one was mine to make. "Because I belong here."

"I don't understand."

So I told him everything. Spilled every drop of my secret, my story. He listened in astonishment as I explained my kinship with nettles, revealed how I was the one summoning shadow around Gizler's store, how the paths and portals shifted for me because of my shadow faery powers. The secret that so many could smell on me was that I was a kind of changeling, in so much as I was a faery left in the human world. How could I have shared it when I didn't know? But the trees had known, the leaflings, and even Pym, which was why she allowed me to ride her.

"So now you know," I said. "It's a long story, but with a happy ending. You finally get to leave."

He gasped shakily, as if he hardly dared believe what I was saying. "I can't just go," he said, shaking his head. "The horses, Morcan."

"I'll happily help Morcan until he can find a replacement for you. A faery, I won't stand to see him snatch a new human servant."

Conor laughed. "Poor Morcan, he doesn't know what he's in for."

"None of them do. I think it's time for the veil between the realms to close, and I intend to make the king and queen see sense. No more stolen children. They owe me that."

"They don't stand a chance," he grinned. Then he fixed me with his most intense stare, more serious than I'd ever seen him. "But what about you? I won't have you."

"You'll have me in here," I promised, pressing my hand to his heart. "Always."

He kissed me then, a sweet and tender first kiss, a painful and sad last kiss, a hello and goodbye all at once.

"I love you," he said.

"I love you too."

As I rested my forehead against his, I pressed a scrap of parchment into his hand. "Please give this to my grandma.

It says everything that needs to be said." A letter telling her that I was safe and home, reunited with my mother. That I knew what she had done and was so grateful. That I would miss her every day of my life to come.

I dug a bracelet from my pocket. "This is for her to wear. For protection." I knew she would, I had seen it in the mirror in town. That had been a glimpse of the future, where my grandma was healed and wearing a bracelet made from nettles. "Remind her to leave me treats, warm milk in the winter, a sprig of lavender in the summer. Ask her to look for me in her dreams, I'll be there to take her hand and walk through the trees. And tell her . . ." My voice broke now. "Tell her I will dance beneath the stars every night and never alone."

He nodded, but still he hesitated. I understood. Once he stepped through the portal, that was it. We would never see each other again.

"Thank you," he said, pulling me close. "For everything." And then, without looking back, he stepped between the trunks and disappeared from sight.

"Goodbye," I whispered, resting my hand against the bark. Then I sat in the dirt and sobbed as though my world had ended.

Under the brilliance of two full moons, the king and queen threw a lavish celebration to mark their happy reunion and all the faeries from both realms danced and drank beneath the scarlet stars.

I struggled to accept that husband and wife could make amends so swiftly after hating each other for so long, but Ellion reminded me that the fae were not like humans. That this was a waltz the king and queen had been dancing for millennia. Years of peace and love, followed by tempestuous estrangement. They always found their way back to each other eventually. And ever since Keita had banished her husband for stealing the faery baby, he had sought a way to return to her, for a way to break through her magic. Thoughts of her had consumed him, even as he'd tried to distract himself with endless merriment. For her part, despite the years Keita had cursed him for taking her precious child, she showed remarkably little interest in that person now they had returned. Her love, it appeared, was as fleeting as the rest. She had loved the idea of a faery baby and nothing more. In the end, I realized all we subjects could do was enjoy this new era of reconciliation while it lasted.

Once we had pledged our loyalty to the king and queen, Ellion and I sneaked away from the festivities. I had something important to do. We walked hand in hand to where the dream-walkers shuffled in their endless torment.

From my pocket, I took more bracelets made from my nettle cloth offcuts, like the one I'd sent home for my grandma. I slipped the first around the wrist of the young servant girl and immediately she stopped moving. A wave of peace passed over her face and I smiled. The bracelets were enough to repel Locryn's enchantment, and though I couldn't free her entirely, at least she would rest from now on.

It didn't take me long to give the remaining dream-walkers their bracelets.

"You have done them a great kindness," Ellion said, looking down at me with affection.

"Perhaps we can convince Locryn and Keita to let them go entirely, but until then, hopefully this will be enough."

Ellion pressed his lips to mine, a kiss that set my body alight. "Will you come with me?" he breathed, his forehead pressed to mine.

"Anywhere," I replied.

He gave me a smile so rare that it was dizzying. He saw me for what I was, he had done for a long time, and he loved me without enchantment or deception. Even so it wasn't enough, I knew that. I had to love what I was too.

He took me into the forest, deep among the trees and shadows, to the glade where I had first seen him in his true form. The trees greeted us, their branches waving in welcome, and I heard their low thrum. Eventually, I would learn to understand them, a prospect which filled me with delight.

I had spent so long torn between my humanity and the stirrings of my faery blood, not knowing where I belonged. It had never occurred to me that I didn't have to choose.

Ellion faced me. "It's time," he said. "Are you ready?"

I nodded, fighting back my fear, as I dared to look inwards. It wasn't easy, learning to truly see myself, harder still to accept it. But I was wild, untamed. Feral and prickly. I was all these things and so much more.

I was Nettle.

A human.

A faery.

A changeling.

I was enough.

At my back, they unfolded, a part of me that I could now embrace. Strong, powerful, beautiful — *mine*.

And I spread my wings wide.

# Acknowledgements

In many ways, the experience of writing this book has been much like being stolen away by the faeries and finding myself lost in a world of beauty and danger. I wrote much of it during a spell of ill health, and disappearing to faery land helped me through many a difficult day. Having lingered there for so long, I'm not sure I've ever really left. And that's okay with me.

As ever, none of this would be possible without the support of an incredible team, all of whom deserve a standing ovation for their brilliance.

My wonderful agent, Davinia Andrew-Lynch, without whom I simply couldn't do any of this.

The amazing Fiona Kennedy — a faery queen disguised as an editor, who believed in *Nettle* from her very first heartbeat.

To all the fantastic Zephyr team—with special thanks to Meg Pickford, Jade Gwilliam, Jo Liddiard, Polly Grice, Zoe Giles, Clemence Jacquinet, and Jessie Price. Thanks also to Felicity Alexander and Hannah Featherstone for their keen eyes.

The excellent EDPR—and especially Sabina Maharjan for her PR prowess.

Endless love and gratitude to Laura El for the most beautiful cover I've ever seen. It literally took my breath away.

Huge thanks to Peter Phillips for taking *Nettle* on another exciting journey, as well as Evan Munday, and all the team at Tundra Books.

All the bookish community, from my fantastic author friends to the exceptional bloggers. Your support means the world to me.

To booksellers—thank you for taking a chance on my books and finding a space on the shelves for them. I'm so grateful. Same goes for librarians and teachers—none of your championing is taken for granted.

And last, but very much not least, my beautiful family. You make everything in my life magical. Thank you.

Bex Hogan
Cambridgeshire
June 2024

# FAERY PLANTS

**1 STINGING NETTLE**
A faery portal

**2 WHITE DEAD NETTLE**
Where the faeries sleep

**3 DANDELION CLOCK**
Faery time

**4 OAK**
One of the oldest faery trees, imparts strength and endurance to those in its aura

### 5 FENNEL
Wards against evil

### 6 MALLOW
Wards against evil

### 7 ASH
A faery abode and one of the most important faery trees alongside oak and thorn

### 8 MEADOWSWEET
Grants second sight and the ability to converse with faeries

### 9 MUGWORT
Associated with midsummer and magic

### 10 WILLOW
A faery abode

Nettle

11 BLUEBELL
Faery flower, witches' thimble

12 WILD THYME
Wards against evil

13 LAVENDER
Summons the faeries on Midsummer's Eve

14 HAWTHORN
A faery portal and a faery abode

15 PRIMROSE
If you eat one, you will be able to see faeries

16 HAZEL
A faery abode

17 FOXGLOVE
Goblin's glove, faery bell, faery cap, faery petticoat

### 18 ROWAN
Protects lost travelers, denoted as a faery tree because of its white blossom

### 19 POPPY
A faery portal which brings faeries into your dreams

### 20 WILD GARLIC
Wards against evil

### 21 GORSE
Offers protection from faeries

### 22 COWSLIP
Or bunch of keys unlock the doors to the Otherworld and hidden faery gold. Also called faery cup as faeries like to curl up in cowslip flowers

### 23 BLACKTHORN
A sacred tree with faery guardians

# Nettle

**24 APPLE**
A faery abode

**25 DAISY**
Grows where faeries tread

**26 DWARF NETTLE**
A faery portal

**SAFFRON**
Cornish flower

All internal images © Shutterstock

Apple: Gaspar Costa, Ash: N_Melanchenko, Blackthorn: umiko, Bluebell: Morphart Creation, Cobweb: Olha Saiuk, Cowslip: FarbaKolerova, Daisy: Morpha, Dandelion: Epine, Dwarf nettle: Hein Nouwens, Feathers: pikepicture, Fennel: Yevheniia Lytvynovych, Foxglove: Yevheniia Lytvynovych, Gorse: Yevheniia Lytvynovych, Hawthorn: Epine, Hawthorn: Morphart Creation, Hazel: Evgenii Doljenkov, Lavender: logaryphmic, Mallow: Yevheniia Lytvynovych, Meadowsweet: Morphart Creation, Moon: Gaspar Costa, Moon: blackstroke, Mugwort: NINA IMAGES, Nettle: Channarong Pherngjanda, Oak: Morphart Creation, Poppy: Yevheniia Lytvynovych, Primrose: Morphart Creation, Rowan: Barashkova Natalia, Saffron: BuKate, Stars: Vlada Young, Thyme: Morphart Creation, White dead nettle: Morphart Creation, Wild garlic: Helena-art, Willow: Hein Nouwens

# OWL KING

SWAN LAKE
MEETS
1001 NIGHTS

COMING
MAY
2026

"Once there was a faery called Ilsette.
She was all things contrary, timid yet bold.
Her voice was the sweetest in the realms.

Once there was a faery called Ilsette.
She was all things tethered and trapped.
Grief had splintered her wings.

Once there was a faery called Ilsette.
She was all things jagged, and sharp with anger.
Fear had left her brittle.

Once there was a faery called Ilsette.
And that faery was me."